THE LONE RANGER
AT THE HAUNTED GULCH

A SUDDEN SHOT SENT THE LONE RANGER AND TONTO
INTO ACTION.

The Lone Ranger at the Haunted Gulch *(Frontispiece Page 35)*

The Lone Ranger
at the Haunted Gulch

Written by FRAN STRIKER

and based on the famous *Lone Ranger* adventures

created by GEO. W. TRENDLE

GROSSET & DUNLAP *Publishers*

NEW YORK

CONTENTS

vi CONTENTS

THE LONE RANGER
AT THE HAUNTED GULCH

THE LONE RANGER
AT THE HAUNTED GULCH

CHAPTER I

A MAN IN TROUBLE

They hanged Rance Morgan at dawn. Over fifty grim-faced men attended the execution, and those fifty shuddered as Morgan, before he stepped into oblivion, cursed and railed at them. Worst of all, was his vow of vengeance, his promise to return from the grave and get his revenge. Impossible as it was, there was an air of conviction about the outlaw's threat. Sheriff Jim Peabody, his deputies, and the men from Kerr's Corners were relieved when the rope jerked and, a moment later, the doctor pronounced Morgan dead.

Two hours after the execution, the burying committee rode back to town and reported to Sheriff Jim Peabody that Rance Morgan had been buried on Boot Hill, near Croyden's Gulch.

Ten hours later, Bat Kester's scrawny form lay lifeless in the cell with marks around his throat that told the story of his death. It was incredible that Rance Morgan could have returned from the grave to strangle the man who had brought about his death, yet every sign supported that theory.

And little did the townspeople of Kerr's Corners dream of the well-laid plot that was designed to make them believe Rance Morgan was dead, of the plot to defeat good common sense and trick them into believing the impossible.

Because of the circumstances, it was necessary that a posse must investigate Croyden's Gulch. Five men, seven horses and a heavy wagon had gone there at Sheriff Peabody's orders only to disappear. Just one of the horses returned to town, and this was ridden by an eyewitness to grim tragedy. From that time the gulch was renamed. It was called the Haunted Gulch.

Many days before he faced the hangman, Rance Morgan had called on Luther Abercrombie, the lawyer.

Abercrombie, a tall man who always dressed in black, was lean, almost emaciated. His cheeks were sunken and his skin, parchmentlike in texture and color, appeared to be stretched tightly over the bones of his face. The sockets of his eyes were so deep that there seemed to be no eyes at all—just empty holes.

Abercrombie sat behind his heavy desk when Rance Morgan entered his office. Morgan glanced about the room, but saw no chair for visitors to use. He turned to the lawyer and spoke nervously. "I—I'm here, Abercrombie, because I need your help."

Abercrombie nodded slowly. "I've been expecting you."

"You have?"

"You've been getting nearer to trouble all the time, Morgan. How long did you think you'd be able to carry on with your gang of cut-throats?" Abercrombie spoke without changing his expression or position. His voice was a dull monotone.

"You said you'd been expectin' me," said Morgan. "What made you think I'd come tuh you? I didn't even think about comin' here until this mornin'."

"I was quite sure that you would become increasingly uneasy with Bat Kester in jail. You well realize that Jim Peabody, the sheriff, has a persuasive manner and you know that Kester is an abject coward. What's to prevent Peabody from convincing Kester that he was sure to hang unless he helped the law put you where *you* belong."

The accuracy of the lawyer's reasoning astonished Rance Morgan.

"You knew," went on the lean-faced man, "that Kester would tell the sheriff all he knew about you. When he did that, Peabody would have proof that you were the one who murdered Jeff Langtree."

"Who says I had anything tuh do with Langtree's death?" demanded Morgan.

"I say so," replied Luther Abercrombie in the same, cool voice.

Rance Morgan shifted his weight uneasily from one foot to the other. He felt ill at ease in the presence of the suave lawyer; he began to believe that Abercrombie had the power to pierce the innermost recesses of his mind and read the things that were there.

"That's neither here nor there," said Morgan defiantly. "What I do, an' what the law can *prove* I do, are two different things."

"Exactly. But if Bat Kester squeals, as he no doubt will, the law will prove that you are a murderer. Of course you are guilty of a lot more than one murder, but the sheriff is interested in finding you guilty *just once*. If he can do that, he will hang you."

Morgan had never been called cowardly, but the cool, deliberate manner in which the lawyer prophesied his fate made him shudder. Again he looked around for a chair.

"I prefer," said Abercrombie slowly, "that men who come to see me stand on their feet."

Rance Morgan looked up sharply. A faint trace of a smile without humor bent the corners of the lawyer's mouth. "You see, Morgan," he said, "I have a fairly good idea of the way your brain works."

"Y-you sure have," muttered Rance Morgan.

"Of course, you want me to take your case if you are placed on trial."

Morgan nodded.

Luther Abercrombie drew from his pocket a small key that was fastened to one end of his watch chain. He fitted this into a lock in one drawer of his desk, opened the drawer and reached inside.

Rance Morgan wondered what was coming next.

Abercrombie held a small black notebook in his hand. His lips pursed slightly as he turned the pages. He leaned forward resting his elbows on the desk and launched into a recital that made Rance Morgan giddy.

The droning voice of Luther Abercrombie seemed like the voice of Morgan's own conscience recalling every detail of his checkered past. Without emotion, the lawyer read off the names of those Morgan himself had killed, then those who had been killed at his command. He read the names of the men who took their orders from the scheming murderer, and read a list of crimes that filled two pages of the notebook. Not only did he itemize each robbery and murder, he stated the amount of profit that had come to Rance Morgan with surprising accuracy.

At first Rance Morgan was tempted to voice loud denials, but he quickly realized their uselessness: Luther Abercrombie knew as much about him as his own conscience. And the lawyer could prove much more troublesome.

When he had finished, Abercrombie put his black book back in the drawer and locked the desk. "I gave you that information," he said, "so you will see the hopelessness of trying to lie to me. If I am to help you, I must have the truth. I also wanted you to know that since I am fully aware of how much cash you are likely to have on hand there is no use telling me my charges are too high."

"All that stuff you got written down there," said Rance Morgan nervously, "it's all mighty lackin' in proof. There ain't a crime there that Sheriff Peabody can prove against me."

"Unless," said Abercrombie with his tight-lipped smile, "Bat Kester decides to do some talking."

Morgan clawed at the bristle of beard on his chin. "Anyhow," he said, "I want you tuh keep me out of jail."

"That's what I assumed. Now we're getting somewhere. Before we discuss anything further, there is a matter of cash that must be settled."

"I ain't called tuh trial yet."

"Not yet, and it will be much easier to keep you out of jail if you never are called to trial."

"Eh?"

"In other words, you pay first! Then we talk."

"How much?"

"To start with, ten thousand dollars."

Rance Morgan began to protest, but the voice of the lawyer continued with quiet persistence smothering his interruption.

"You lay ten thousand dollars on the corner of this desk and then we will go into details about your future security."

"For that cash you'll keep me out of jail?"

"I may require more before we have finished. We'll have to see how things turn out."

While Morgan pondered, Luther Abercrombie tilted back in his chair and, ignoring the visitor in the office, read from a leather-covered book.

"All right," snapped Rance Morgan. "I need you an' I've got tuh pay. I'll have that cash here before noon."

If Luther Abercrombie had known the background of a stranger who was camped outside of town at that very moment, if he had known the purpose of the stranger and the Indian who traveled with him to the neighborhood of Kerr's Corners, he would have felt far less confident of keeping Rance Morgan a free man.

The Lone Ranger and Tonto had arrived.

CHAPTER II

A MEAL TO KILL

It took an incredibly short time for the Lone Ranger and Tonto to establish the camp that might be their home for many days. While the Indian built a small lean-to, the masked man unpacked the saddlebags and sougans.

Their site was chosen with the greatest care. It was surrounded by dense woods with an almost perpendicular wall on one side. A small cascade gave the men and horses an unlimited supply of clear water for washing and drinking. Flat stones from the bottom of a stream were fashioned into a fireplace so cunningly designed that, even after dark, the flames could not be seen twenty paces beyond the camp.

The Lone Ranger and Tonto had ridden to the place when stories of the depredations and murders in Kerr's Corners reached their ears.

The masked man knew Jim Peabody by reputation. He knew that as a sheriff, Peabody was sincere and tireless. He also knew that the lawman was physically unable to be very active.

"We'll go there and see what's going on," the Lone Ranger had told Tonto.

When the camp was nearly settled the Lone Ranger gave his Indian friend instructions.

8

The Lone Ranger was an almost legendary character. His adventures furnished material for countless stories around the campfires and in the cabins of seven states. Very little was known about him. No one could describe his face because his face had never been seen. Although he generally wore a mask, at times he disguised himself with stains that Tonto prepared from roots and berries.

He seemed to be goaded on an endless trail, striving constantly to go wherever there was crime or oppression that couldn't be handled by man-made laws. Only one man in the world knew the Lone Ranger; that man was Tonto the Indian.

People thought the solid silver bullets the Lone Ranger used were sheer extravagance, but there was a definite reason for them. The Lone Ranger had pledged himself never to take a life. When he fired, it was in defense of his own life or the life of someone else. At these times he fired to wound—not to kill. He fired to blast away the gun of an opponent. Lead bullets striking the tempered steel of another man's gun might spatter and send dangerous fragments flying. Bullets of silver would not do this.

There were many rumors concerning the source of the masked man's income. Some people claimed he was an outlaw; others that he collected rewards for the criminals he jailed. Both of these conjectures were far from the truth.

The truth was surprisingly simple. The Lone Ranger

could have been a wealthy man if he had chosen a different life. He owned a silver mine, but preferred his roaming existence in the hills and valleys and his long rides on the plains. No one but Tonto knew about the silver mine. When there was need to do so, Tonto would disappear for several days. On his return he would have gathered and sold enough of the precious ore to carry the two companions on their way for many weeks.

The Lone Ranger knew that self-preservation was nature's first law. He also knew that the wild beasts of the forest interpreted that law without greed or dishonesty. It was these traits in men which disgusted the masked rider and which he sought to suppress. Animal law was based on the things that were best for the greatest number. That same principle was the foundation of the Lone Ranger's justice.

Some men—Rance Morgan for example—went unpunished only because of legal technicalities in manmade laws. Jim Peabody must be at his wit's end in his efforts to put Morgan behind bars. Everyone knew that Rance was a killer. No one could prove it.

The Lone Ranger was deep in thoughts and plans while he inspected his equipment. Bat Kester, he knew, was in jail. Bat might talk, but surely Rance Morgan would anticipate this. What would Morgan do about it?

It was vital that the masked man learn all he could about conditions in Kerr's Corners. It was equally important that he do this as secretly as possible. He in-

ventoried the elements that had gone into the forma-
tion of his decision to send Tonto into town alone.

He had the utmost faith in Tonto's ability to observe
and read correctly the motives and actions of Kester,
Morgan, the sheriff, and any others concerned. Then,
too, an Indian arriving in town was generally given
no more attention than might be paid a stray dog. A
white man, on the other hand, would be the object of
close scrutiny by everyone, and the natural curiosity
of the westerner would make the townsmen restless
until they had learned the identity of the stranger.

Tonto's horse, a paint called Scout, was far superior
to the smaller mustangs that were ridden by most
Indians, but it would take a keen observer to spot the
sterling qualities of Scout if Tonto chose to hide them.
Scout was second only to the powerful white stallion
ridden by the Lone Ranger himself—the mighty Silver.

Tonto covered the stretch of open country between
the town and the woods at high speed. His style of riding was unorthodox; a combination of the Indians'
high-elbowed form and the Texas cowboy's slump. As
he approached Kerr's Corners he reined Scout to a
slow walk. He drew a blanket about his shoulders and
assumed a drooping posture that would indicate
fatigue.

Through eyes that were half-closed the Indian noticed the men he rode past on the one street in town.
No one cast a second look in his direction.

Tonto slipped to the ground at the hitch rack in

front of Prindle's general store and tossed Scout's reins about the heavy wooden rail. His sharp eyes took in a great deal in a few quick glances. He saw Rance Morgan and recognized the killer. Morgan was stepping across the porch in front of Jim Peabody's office.

Morgan held a package in his hand.

Tonto shuffled slowly toward the building where the weather-beaten sign said *Jim Peabody, Sheriff*. He opened the door a few seconds after Morgan had gone through it.

Jim Peabody looked up. His voice was almost as big and impressive as his stomach. Peabody was notoriously fat. It had been ten years since the sheriff had ridden a horse and his stomach bulged in a way that made the lawman look almost as broad as he was tall. In fact it was said that the sheriff would reach higher if he were on his back.

"What d'you want?" boomed Peabody looking at Tonto.

"Me want talk," replied the Indian.

"Wait outside then, I'm busy now."

Tonto nodded and retreated through the door. This was just exactly what he had hoped would happen. Now he had a perfectly logical excuse for sitting on the porch and tuning his keen ear to the conversation inside between the sheriff and Rance Morgan. He heard Morgan speaking:

"You've got a friend of mine locked up, Jim."

"Is Bat Kester a friend of yores?"

"Sure he is."

"Then I don't think much of yore friends. Kester is a killer an' he's due to hang. Mebbe the only difference between you an' him is that he's been *proved* a killer."

Tonto noticed the emphasis on the word "proved" and heard the angry growl that came from Rance Morgan in reply.

"Anyhow," continued the sheriff, "what about it? Bat ain't havin' no visitors."

"All I wanted to do was take him some eatin' tobacco," explained Rance Morgan. "Him an' me used tuh be good friends before he went bad. I sort of hate tuh see Bat waitin' for his hangin' without a chew of tobacco tuh help lift his droppin' spirits."

"Anything you got for the prisoner will have tuh be sent in with his grub. Take the tobacco across the street tuh my wife an' tell her it's to go in the bundle when she sends his next meal over tuh him."

"All right, Sheriff, if that's the way you want it."

"That's the way it's goin' tuh be, Morgan. I know that you are plumb scared thinkin' Bat Kester might squeal on a few things that would get you in trouble. I wouldn't put it past you tuh fill him with lead if you got in shootin' range."

"You must think I'm all kinds of a fool tuh try shootin' a prisoner while you're sittin' here."

"I think you're anything *but* a fool. You'd shoot, then produce a dozen men that'd swear you was fifty miles from here at the time of the shootin'! It'd be my word against the word of a dozen pals of yours an' you'd go scot-free like you've done before. Now git out o' here, Morgan. Yuh make the air unfit tuh breathe!"

The door opened the next moment and Rance Morgan brushed past Tonto without noticing him.

Dust puffed from the road with each step Rance Morgan took. Tonto watched him cross the road and go toward the rear of a small house with clapboard sides that had been painted white. The Morgan fist that had frequently gripped death-spitting guns rapped on the kitchen door.

Ma Peabody answered. When she saw Rance Morgan her mouth compressed until it was a lipless line. "What d'you want?" she demanded coldly.

Morgan followed the procedure as outlined by the lawyer. He had spent ten thousand dollars to secure the pattern of his scheme and he didn't propose to have that money wasted.

"Your husband told me tuh come here," he said as he removed his hat. "I've got a pack of tobacco here for the prisoner. I'm supposed tuh put it with the grub you're fixin' for him."

"Do so then," replied the white-haired woman. "I'm busy fixin' it right now. Put it there on the table."

Morgan nodded, suppressing his satisfaction. His visit had been timed perfectly. Abercrombie had explained that Ma Peabody was a creature of habit, one could tell the time of day by what the woman did. At precisely the same hour each day she prepared food when there was a prisoner in the jail. The food basket, half-filled, was on the table in the kitchen.

While the lawman's wife muttered disapproval of the "disgustin' vile habit of eatin' t'bacco," Rance crossed the room and dropped the packet in the basket. He did something else. In the palm of his hand he held a thimble slightly less than half-filled with small white crystals. Unobtrusively, he lifted the lid from a bowl of steaming beef stew and let the powder spill among the vegetables. It looked like salt.

"Well, stop your nosin' around there an' clear out," the wife of the sheriff said. "Soon's the coffee boils I've got to take that basket out."

"Thanks for lettin' me send my friend the present," Rance said.

Ma Peabody didn't reply.

Morgan left the house well pleased with his manner of handling things. "Now," he muttered, "Bat Kester won't do no talkin' about me or anyone else. I sure have tuh hand it tuh Abercrombie. He has the right idea. Defend a man *before* he's called tuh trial."

Five minutes later the basket of food was carried to the sheriff's office. Whoever ate the stew or used the tobacco would imbibe a dose of deadly poison.

CHAPTER III

A CHARGE OF MURDER

Ma Peabody strode into her husband's office with the air of a martyr and the voice of a harridan.

"Sweatin' an' slavin' over a red-hot stove to fix hot meals for a no-account, murderin' polecat," she complained. "Cold wild turkey is good enough for you an' me to eat, but when it comes to fixin' vittles for a prisoner them things won't do. No sir, ordinary eatin' ain't good enough for a prisoner. The law says we got to feed him hot food. It don't make sense."

Jim Peabody was familiar with these outbursts. He looked up and grinned at his wife. "One thing I always liked about you, Sara," he said. "You aint lackin' none in spunk."

"Nothin' but a lot of doggone foolishness," the woman retorted. "Here's a coyote that's due to hang. We'd be savin' him a mighty sore throat if we was to let him starve, but the law says we can't do that. We got to feed him. We got to fix hot vittles for the side-winder."

"We get paid by the county for his grub, Sara, now just you ca'm down. Leave the food there an' I'll take it tuh him."

Sara had already left the food and was halfway to the door when the sheriff finished speaking. She snatched the door open, turned and said, "I'd like to see him choke on that there food." Sara slammed the door behind her.

Jim Peabody eyed the basket wistfully. The aroma that rose from the beef stew caressed his nostrils and kept him swallowing rapidly to dispose of the saliva that came in response to the fragrance. He sighed deeply. "Time was," he mused, "when I could eat that sort of food."

The delightful blending of good beef, onions, potatoes, parsnips and turnip that scented the steam was tempting to the flies as well as the big man. They buzzed around the stew and kept Peabody's big hand waving.

"Proud woman," he muttered with reference to his wife. "Even when she's doin' cookin' fer a man she'd like tuh see choke on the grub, she has tuh make it smell like nectar from the gods."

He glanced at the big stomach that had caused the doctor to taboo a meal at noon and reflected that he might rightfully blame his bulk on Sara. The sheriff was in no hurry to rid his office of the perfume. He couldn't eat, but there was no doctor on earth who could place a ban on smelling.

He was so absorbed in a study of the prisoner's repast that he didn't hear the opening and closing of his office door. It wasn't until Tonto addressed him by name that he was aware of another presence in the office.

"Peabody!" The name was spoken in a heavy voice.

The lawman turned as quickly as he could, his chair protesting loudly. He stared in surprise at the Indian before him; then in anger at the gun the Indian held.

"What's this mean," Peabody bellowed.

"You stay in chair," replied Tonto.

The sheriff remained motionless, studying the man in front of him. "What d'you want here?" he inquired.

Tonto holstered his gun and advanced to the desk. "You got food here," he said.

The lawman nodded.

"Tonto show what happen when man eat food."

Fascinated by the odd manner of the tall Indian, Jim Peabody said nothing. Tonto took the lid from the stew. Once more the steam arose. Then he dipped a finger into the thick mass and daubed a few drops of the gravy on the desk top.

In his jerky manner of speech Tonto told the sheriff what had happened in the kitchen a few minutes before. He explained that he had just happened to see Rance Morgan there. He told how Rance had dropped white powder into the stew while Sara's back was turned. Then Tonto halted.

A fly landed on the desk top near the drops of gravy. For a moment the insect rubbed its front legs together, then advanced a step.

Tonto spoke softly. "Not make-um move now. Watch-um closely."

The fly came close to the food and halted as if to inspect and examine the discovery.

"You mean tuh say," breathed Jim Peabody, "that Morgan put poison in that grub?"

"Watch-um fly."

The fly reached the drops of gravy and started eating. Now other flies were on the desk. Jim Peabody could scarcely believe his eyes. Fly number one jerked back, its legs quite stiff. For a moment the wings of the insect fluttered and then stilled. The sheriff drew a pencil from the pocket of his vest and nudged the motionless insect. "Dead!"

Tonto nodded slowly.

"Rance Morgan's poisoned that there food."

Instead of replying, Tonto picked up the chewing tobacco and held it closer to the window. Tiny crystalline flakes could be seen adhering to the surface of the weed.

"So that's the polecat's scheme. He figgered Bat Kester would squeal on him. He aimed tuh pizen him before he got around tuh tellin' anything."

Jim Peabody rose from his chair. He brushed Tonto to one side and grabbed up the basket of food.

"I'm callin' on the one man in these parts that knows the law," he bellowed. "If this ain't attempted murder, I'm a heathen Chinee. If I can't jail Rance Morgan for attempted murder then I don't know the first golblasted thing about the law."

He slapped the door open and strode ponderously out of the office ignoring the fact that Tonto, if he chose to do so, could have let the prisoner free.

Bat Kester stood in his cell, his face white and drawn at what he had heard and seen between the bars.

"Tried tuh murder me, the skunk," he said weakly. "Well, now, my mind's made up. I'll tell enough tuh hang Rance Morgan ten times over!"

Tonto grinned and sat down in the sheriff's chair. "Me stay here," he said. "Tonto see you not die before you talk."

It was an hour later when Jim Peabody returned, his face hot and red, with sweat dripping from his forehead. Tonto rose and surrendered the sheriff's chair.

"I reckon I owe you a vote of thanks," Jim said to Tonto when he breathed normally. "If it hadn't been fer you, my prisoner would o' died an' I'd o' been the laughin' stock of everyone around here. It might even have been worse. Mr. Abercrombie tells me that there might even have been charges of murder put ag'in my wife."

Tonto nodded that he understood what the big sheriff said.

"I reckon if anyone around here knows the law, it's Luther Abercrombie. I figgered fer sure that I'd be able tuh jail Morgan fer attemptin' this yere murder, but Abercrombie tells me that I'd just waste my time tryin' tuh make the charges stick. No one was pizened, an' no one but you know about Rance puttin' that powder in the food. There'd be you tryin' tuh tell the truth against a dozen men that'd swear that Rance was somewheres else at the time you claim he was in Sara's kitchen."

Tonto listened patiently, aware that the sheriff was talking more to clarify the matter in his own mind than to impart any information. Now Tonto spoke. "Morgan feller not get-um punishment?"

Peabody shook his head. "Hain't nothin' I can prove." He hesitated and then a new expression came into his broad face. "But maybe there is!" He gained his feet once more and went close to the barred door.

"You—Bat Kester," the lawman called.

The man addressed rose slowly from his bunk and came up to the bars of his door.

"You seen an' heard what happened in here, Kester?" Bat nodded. "I seen it."

"You know now what chance you got of stayin' alive even if you don't talk. The best thing you can do is tuh tell enough on Rance Morgan so I can jail the rat an' get him where he won't have another chance at you!"

Bat Kester said, "He—he'll sure as thunder kill me if I squeal."

"He'll kill you if you don't. An' if you don't squeal, an' Rance don't kill you, you'll hang anyhow. I'm givin' you the chance tuh get a term in the state prison instead of hangin'. Now don't be too addlebrained to take what I'm offerin' you."

Tonto studied the prisoner's face and slipped silently from the room. The Indian, keen student of human nature that he was, hadn't the slightest doubt in his mind: the more Bat Kester pondered on the sheriff's proposition the more certain he would be to talk.

It was simply a matter of time before Rance Morgan would be picked up by Peabody's willing deputies and lodged in jail to await trial.

Marie are just ordinary men.

Besides they had more common sense. If nothing
more, the same

CHAPTER IV

THE SHERIFF GETS HIS MAN

Two men strode, side by side, along the dusty street
until they reached Rance Morgan's favorite saloon.
They turned in at the swinging doors of Pete's Place.

"There he is," muttered the taller of the two.

The other nodded.

Rance Morgan toyed with his half-filled glass of
whiskey making wet rings on the polished surface of
the bar. He didn't notice either of the deputies until
they stood next to him, one on each side. He glanced
first at one, and then the other.

"Seems tuh me," he observed, "Sheriff Peabody
must've changed his style. I didn't know he let his men
drink while they were on duty."

"He don't," the short man said briefly.

"Oh." A pause. "I take it you ain't on duty then. I'd
admire buyin' you two gents a drink. Name your
pizen."

"Where," drawled the tall man softly, "did you get
the idea we wasn't on duty?" His hand dropped to his
belt with his fingers less than an inch from the butt of
his gun.

"Rance," said the other, "you finish your drink; then
come along with us. Take your time because this'll

23

likely be the last drink you'll have for some time. Maybe the last one for all time."

Rance Morgan had never been lacking in confidence and poise. But now, the knowledge that Luther Abercrombie was working in his behalf made him feel that he could overcome practically anything that the lawmen in Kerr's Corners might bring against him. He grinned easily at the men beside him.

"That fool sheriff is gettin' tuh be a regular pest," he said. "Every so often he gets a notion that I'm a crook of some sort an' then I have tuh spend an hour or so convincin' him that he's mistaken."

"I don't figure he's made a mistake this time," the tall man with the badge of office said.

"No?"

The deputy shook his head. "Drink up an' come along quiet."

"I always thought a man was told why he was arrested. Is it a secret or something?"

"It's no secret, Morgan. The sheriff wants you for the murder of Flint Murdock."

Flint Murdock! If Peabody knew about *that* murder, it could only be through Bat Kester.

"Where did Peabody get the idea I had anything tuh do with Murdock's death?"

"He's got a pretty airtight case against you, Rance. I don't know as you'll be able to beat the law this time. Fact is, I'd hate like thunder to be in the spot you're in right now."

The grim manner of the deputies should have worried Rance Morgan but it didn't. His interview with Luther Abercrombie had given him such confidence in his high-priced legal counsel that he took his arrest with complete unconcern. He recalled all that Abercrombie had said. "We'll try to fix it so Kester won't be able to talk. If we fail in that, we'll manage in someway to have the jury find you not guilty. If, by some odd twist of circumstance, you are charged with murder and found guilty, there are still some tricks left in the bag. Don't worry. My clients are never punished."

Morgan tossed off the remainder of his drink and set the glass down on the bar. He slid a coin toward the aproned man and turned with a patronizing air toward the deputy on his right.

"Let's get started," Morgan said. "The sooner we call on the sheriff, the sooner this will be over with."

Neither of the lawmen made a comment. The trio left the saloon, Rance Morgan walking between the others. It was a matter of two minutes walk to reach Jim Peabody's office.

The sheriff looked unpleasant, his mood was ugly.

Rance Morgan fancied that his smile might be disarming, but he was doomed to disappointment.

"I got nothin' at all to say," the sheriff growled. "You men throw that rat in the jail an' bring Bat Kester out."

"C'mon," the tall deputy growled as he gripped one arm of the captive.

"Hold on, why ain't you goin' tuh keep Kester in jail?"

"It's none of your business what we do with him," the sheriff barked. "We don't aim tuh give you another chance tuh kill the prisoner, so we're movin' him."

"I don't know what you're talking about. Another chance to kill him? What do you mean?"

"Throw him in the jug," Peabody ordered, ignoring Morgan's question.

Rance Morgan felt that there should be more formality to his arrest. He should at least have the chance to discuss the matter. After all, he was looked upon in town as a man of influence. It was hardly fitting that he should be accorded treatment that might be given a vagrant or a whiskey-soaked Indian. Resentment was rising up within him, dictating angry comments, but they went unvoiced. His lawyer had warned him that he *might* be arrested and had cautioned him to say nothing. Abercrombie had made an impression that was so deep it stifled anything that Morgan might have said.

Bat Kester glowered black hatred at Rance Morgan in the brief moment that the two men were in the cell together. "Try tuh kill me, will you?" he growled before the deputies had escorted him out of the cell and slammed the door on Morgan.

Jim Peabody gave instructions for the disposal of Bat Kester. He was to be held under guard in a spare room in the sheriff's own home until Rance Morgan had been tried. "It won't take long tuh find him guilty, an' we'll hold the hangin' right soon after the trial, then Kester can have his cell back again."

The sheriff did not wait to see his orders carried out. He left the office and, with his ponderous gait, barged toward the office of the lawyer.

Big Jim did not know that Luther Abercrombie had a strictly private policy and a mode of conduct that he told no one about.

It is a well-known and much-used figure of speech that some men play "both ends against the middle." Luther Abercrombie went beyond that: he played a dozen spokes against the hub. He himself was the hub.

While he connived in the interest of Rance Morgan —for ten thousand dollars—he acted the part of counselor and generous advisor to win the good will of the sheriff. He would need the sheriff's good will. Big Jim trusted him and he wanted to maintain the status quo.

When he saw Jim Peabody head toward his office, a tight little smile played on Abercrombie's lips. He opened the door for the sheriff. "I saw you take your prisoner into custody," he said by way of greeting.

"Yup. We got him all right, Mister Abercrombie, and he didn't put up the argument I thought he might."

"You are taking my advice, though?"

"Oh, sure. I ain't goin' tuh make a fool of myself by chargin' him with tryin' tuh pizen Bat Kester. Fact is, I don't need to. I can hang the skunk for a murder that didn't fizzle out."

"Indeed?" Abercrombie's lifted eyebrows registered surprise. He acted as though he hadn't heard a word about any murder Kester could prove against Rance Morgan.

"That's why I came here, Mister Abercrombie. I wanted to speak to you about Rance Morgan."

The lawyer nodded, and glowed with inward pride that he was addressed as "Mister" by the sheriff.

"I understand that yore tuh be his lawyer."

Abercrombie nodded with great dignity. "It is unfortunate," he sighed, "that we of the legal profession must serve humanity with the same meticulous care that characterizes men who devote their lives to healing the sick or ministering to men's immortal souls."

Peabody squinted slightly and said, "Huh?"

"Men come to us in their trouble and it is not for us to choose. We must serve where we are needed. This man Morgan has the right of every man to his day in court. He is innocent until he has been proved guilty. He has the right to legal counsel and he has retained me."

"Yuh mean, he paid yuh to git him off this murder charge?"

"Like many others, Sheriff Peabody, you have a misconception of a lawyer's duty. It is my duty to see that my client is given a just and fair trial, to present his side of the case and his reason for the murder, if he has one. It will be for a jury of his peers to determine whether or not he shall be judged guilty or not guilty.

I will resort to no deceit in court. Neither will I conceal or attempt to distort the facts of the case. If my client is guilty, he shall pay the penalty as decided by the court."

Jim Peabody listened to the lawyer with his head slightly tilted to one side; he grasped the general idea of what the man was saying and let it go at that. Though he wished Abercrombie would talk in more simple language, it was not for him to say so.

"I sort of get the idea from what yuh say that you ain't goin' to ruin yer own reputation by bein' too anxious tuh git this killer free. Is that it?"

"The facts must speak for themselves."

"That'll suit me just fine," replied the sheriff. He added significantly, "the last lawyer that settled here was too ambitious. He even went so far as tuh try an' buy the jury tuh git a man that was downright unpopular out of a horse stealin' charge. What d'you think happened tuh him?"

Abercrombie shook his head without speaking.

"Well, Mister Abercrombie, he was treated tuh a bath in hot tar, then given a dressin' of feathers and a free ride out of town on a rail."

"He must have been guilty," said the lawyer, "of gross carelessness."

Jim Peabody nodded. "He sure was."

"I think," said Luther Abercrombie, "we understand each other perfectly. My client anticipated trouble when he heard that you were eager to jail him. That was why he retained me. Now that he is jailed, it is up to you to prove him guilty of murder. I give you my word that, for my part, the trial will be a fair one."

"That," said the sheriff, "is all I'm askin'." He turned toward the door, advanced toward it, but halted and looked back.

"I figured you fer a smart man, Mister Abercrombie. I guess I figured right. Some time when you're not busy, stop at my house an' I'll show you the fence rail they used when the last lawyer decided tuh leave town."

CHAPTER V

GUNPLAY AT NIGHT

Tonto rode into the cleverly concealed camp with word of Rance Morgan's arrest. While the Lone Ranger listened attentively the Indian supplied details about the evidence Bat Kester had given the sheriff; he reported the unconcern with which the killer had accepted his arrest and the confident manner he displayed throughout the entire proceeding. From time to time, the Lone Ranger broke in with a question. When Tonto finished his recital of the facts the mystery rider rose to his feet.

"If he took his capture so calmly," the Lone Ranger decided, "he must have some sort of scheme. Rance Morgan has at least a dozen and perhaps more than a score of men who are ready to do his bidding. Morgan can tell enough to cause the arrest and hanging of practically every member of his gang. Those men will go to any extreme to get him out of jail."

Tonto nodded.

While the Lone Ranger spoke, he paced slowly back and forth. "This is a time when there's little that I can do. Once more you'll have to be the one who goes into Kerr's Corners. You've made a friend of Sheriff Peabody; that's to our advantage."

"What Tonto do now?"

"I want you to go back to town and keep a close watch on Rance Morgan. Watch him every moment of the time even though he's locked behind iron bars."

"Tonto do that."

"Come back here every evening and tell me who calls on Morgan at the jail, make a note of everything that is said, if you can hear the discussions, and see that no written messages are exchanged between Morgan and his men outside. I want to know who Morgan's friends are."

Tonto sat reflectively for several minutes while his deep, dark eyes looked fixedly at the glowing coals in the small campfire. "There one thing," he muttered at length.

"What's that?"

"Morgan not act right."

The Lone Ranger waited in silence for the Indian to enlarge upon the cryptic statement.

"Morgan not get mad. Morgan not have lot to say. Him not act like feller should."

"I think I know what you mean, Tonto, and the reason I'm so sure that Morgan's planning an escape is simply because of the way he's behaving. If he didn't have a few tricks up his sleeve he'd be pretty hard to handle. We're going to stick close to town until that killer gets all that's coming to him, and if he makes a play to break out of jail—well, there might be need for a faster horse than any animal in town." He paused and glanced toward the trees where Silver was tethered. "We have that kind of horse."

A soft breeze stirred the leafy roof of the Lone Ranger's camp. The gentle and contented-sounding clump of the neat, hard hoofs of Scout and Silver and the soft crackling of the resinous wood in the fire were the only sounds to intrude themselves on the two friends who sat with their blankets drawn about their shoulders, each lost in private thought.

There was an understanding between the Lone Ranger and Tonto that had grown from the deeply imbedded roots of their friendship. They understood each other so completely that they could sit in camp or ride the trail for hours without the exchange of a spoken word. Yet there was a constant exchange of thoughts, each man seemed to sense just what the other was thinking.

Tonto, sitting silently in the camp, was fully aware that the masked man had started on a new crusade. He had ridden to the country surrounding Kerr's Corners because of a long list of crimes that were seemingly without solution. The arrest of Rance Morgan might, if the trial and execution went forward without a hitch, remove one desperado from the picture. But one only. There were others, no one knew how many. Until every member of Rance Morgan's well-knit gang was brought to justice, Kerr's Corners would not be the sort of place it should be, the sort of place the Lone Ranger wanted the entire West to be.

If Tonto had been educated in the white men's schools where there were books about the knights of old, he might have seen the close bond between the tall, strong man who wore the mask and the armored, helmetted riders of old who had restlessly traveled through the world in search of the Holy Grail.

The Lone Ranger at the moment was relaxed. That is, he was as relaxed as he ever could be, knowing that constant vigilance was the price he must pay for security. In this relaxation he stored up energy. Before the present quest of justice came to an end there might be need of the last ounce of the strength the masked man possessed. There might be days and nights without the chance to rest; battles in which his life would be forfeit if he lost.

Tonto rose to his feet and moved close to the fire. He squatted there and poked among the coals with a small stick, pushing ashes close to the embers. A tiny shower of sparks rose up among the treetops and for a moment the flames burned brighter.

Abruptly the Indian grew tense. Silver too sensed something foreign in the dark forest. The intelligent horse, so carefully trained by his masked master, sounded a warning by pawing ever so softly on the ground.

Instinctively the Lone Ranger snatched his gun and half-turned toward the horses. Silence, then the sharp snap of a breaking twig. No animal made a sound like that. There was a man, or men, in the woods near by.

Tonto strained every faculty to penetrate the silence and darkness, and to determine the direction from which the sound had come. Someone must have followed the Indian from town. But why? A sudden shot sent them into action.

A bullet bit into a log almost before the crack of the gun was heard. Tonto caught a brief flash of flame far back among the trees. He was on his feet and running.

The Lone Ranger, too, leaped up. He cut sharply to one side, plunged among the trees, then raced toward the spot where the gun's flame had been seen. He and Tonto converged in the darkness, but the man who had fired upon them could be heard beating a fast and reckless retreat.

"He's going that way," the Lone Ranger said.

The two plunged through the darkness following the sound of running feet. The fugitive had thrown all caution to the wind and was making no effort to keep his flight secret.

The edge of the woods was not far away. The running man broke from the trees while Tonto and the Lone Ranger were less than fifty feet behind him. He made a fine target, the unknown, but no shot was fired. Instead of pushing on, the Lone Ranger and Tonto halted abruptly and watched. A group of men and horses were waiting for the gunman.

Sharp cries came from the group. "Grab him," someone shouted above the others.

The fugitive stopped and half-turned to retreat into

the woods, but it was too late, three men were upon him instantly and bore him to the ground.

Tonto gripped the strong arm of the tall masked man and whispered softly. "Moonlight show-um feller. Tonto know-um."

"Who is he?"

The answer came from beyond the trees in the voice of a deputy sheriff. "Try to escape will you, Kester? Well, this time we'll keep a closer watch on you."

"Bat Kester?" whispered the Lone Ranger.

"That right."

Kester's voice was high-pitched and almost hysterical.

"That Indian," he cried. "He's the same as murdered me. I had the chance tuh get out of that place where you put me an' I follered him. He's got a friend in that there woods. He framed me tuh git killed."

A man said, "Kester, you're just plain loco."

"I ain't nothin' of the kind. I know what I'm talkin' about. I seen the way Rance Morgan looked at me when he was put intuh the jail in my place. That man'll kill me fer squealin' on him, I know he will."

"Rance Morgan's killin' days are over. He goes on trial next week, an' he'll hang."

"He'll kill me," declared Kester who seemed, in his abject fear, to be beyond the point of reason. "I know he will. It was that Injun that framed it all. I thought it over an' I know what I'm talkin' about."

"Get some ropes on him an' take that gun away," a curt voice said.

As the two watched from the cover of the friendly trees, the soft light of the moon showed Bat Kester being disarmed and roped.

Kester continued to babble wildly as his hands were being tied. "Sheriff Peabody was bound and determined tuh make me tell what I knew about Rance Morgan. It was him tipped that Indian off tuh make out that the grub for me was pizened by Rance Morgan. Then he told me how it was a case of me tellin' all I knew, or getting bumped off by Morgan. So I squealed. Peabody got what he wanted before I had the chance tuh think it over. Now Morgan'll get me."

A heavy voice broke in, "Don't be a darn fool, Kester, if you'll use your head, you'll realize that you were slated for hanging until you squealed. Now you'll get off with a few years in jail. And Morgan can't do no murder after he's dead."

"Rance Morgan'll get me! I know he will!" Kester didn't realize how prophetic he was. "If he don't get me before he hangs, he'll get me *after!*"

"Loco!" commented a deputy. "The poor galoot's gone loco. I'd sure like tuh know how Morgan does it. He's got this critter scairt tuh death of him."

The men with the recaptured Bat Kester mounted their horses after hoisting the fugitive upon the horse he had left outside of the woods. In another moment they were returning to Kerr's Corners at a gallop.

"They seem to have ignored what Kester told them about us, Tonto," the Lone Ranger said.

Tonto did not reply. The two returned to their camp, but remained only long enough to pack their duffel and extinguish the remains of the fire. Caution dictated that they go deeper into the woods where the masked man would wait while Tonto spent the next few days in town.

CHAPTER VI

THE TRIAL

When Tonto entered the sheriff's office on the day after Bat Kester's escape and recapture, Jim Peabody lost no time in asking about the white man whom the Indian had met in the woods.

"Jack Tilson, he's my deputy, claims that Kester saw you with this hombre an' accordin' tuh Kester's story he was masked. What about it, Tonto?"

Tonto nodded.

"You admit it, eh?" Peabody leaned back, his chair squeaking with the strain. "You done me a good turn, Indian," he said slowly. "If it hadn't been fer you, Kester would've been dead an' Rance Morgan would still be free. Now I'm willin' to be downright partial toward you, but I have tuh know what's goin' on."

Once more Tonto nodded. "That right," he said.

"Who is this masked man?"

The Indian reached a hand into the pocket of his buckskin jacket and brought out a small object. He held this for the lawman to see. "You know what this mean?" he said.

Peabody picked up the cartridge and examined it casually at first and then with a critical eye. "Shiny," he muttered. He set his teeth on the brightly polished

39

bullet then studied it again. He looked questioningly at Tonto.

"Bullet made of silver," said the Indian.

"Silver?"

A nod. "Masked man ride horse name Silver."

For a moment the sheriff looked puzzled. His broad brow became a mass of furrows as he tried to correlate the things the Indian had said. Then his expression brightened and his brow went smooth. "Do you mean," he said softly, "that this masked friend that's in the woods is the gent I've heard about? Tell me," he leaned forward tensely, "is it the Lone Ranger?"

Tonto smiled proudly and his head went down and up in a single nod.

"Well, I'll be—" The sheriff wiped a hand across his sweating face. "I'll be hanged! I've heard about the Lone Ranger. I've heard that there ain't nothin' like him ever lived, but I never expected tuh *see* him."

"You not see him yet," said Tonto.

"But he's near here. He's in the woods. Why, jumpin' juniper, maybe he'll even *help* me if he knows I need him."

The sheriff felt a surging of suppressed excitement. Again he breathed the words "The Lone Ranger."

Tonto had won the sheriff's good will and he made the most of it. He spent his time in close proximity to the jail, some of the time in the office of the sheriff. He watched constantly for men to come and speak to Rance Morgan. With the patience characteristic of his race, he waited for some sign of communication between the prisoner awaiting trial and the men who *must* be planning to help him. Yet he saw no contact between Rance Morgan and the world beyond his bars.

Morgan's manner through the entire week was baffling to both Tonto and the sheriff, but it only confirmed a suspicion that had been growing in the Lone Ranger's mind.

"Abercrombie," the Lone Ranger told Tonto in one of the conferences the two held each night, "is one of the sharpest, shrewdest men I've ever heard of. He has probably told Morgan to remain quiet until the trial. He isn't guilty of the murder until it has been proved in court. If Morgan makes any attempt to escape, the guards at the prison would have every right to shoot him. As long as he behaves himself he can demand a fair trial. If, at the trial, he's proved guilty of murder that will be soon enough for an attempt to rescue him."

Tonto didn't relax his vigilance in spite of what the masked man had said. And he was especially watchful on the two occasions when Luther Abercrombie called at the jail to confer with his client. At last came the day of the trial. The small courthouse was packed until it fairly bulged at the walls. The air was stifling. No one suspected that the Lone Ranger himself was one of the spectators.

Although the mystery rider attended Morgan's trial unmasked, he wore a disguise that had often enabled him to pass unnoticed in a crowd. A small mustache and bushy eyebrows fastened by spirit gum together with the cunningly applied stains that Tonto made out of roots completely changed his appearance.

The Lone Ranger had left his brace of guns and the belts of silver bullets behind and wore only one rather battered-looking gun, which could be handed in to the guard at the courtroom door. His always immaculate clothing had been discarded in favor of patched and dust-laden flannel shirt and dungarees, his white stetson had given way to a nondescript hat of dingy felt with a brim that drooped despondently in old age.

Court opened.

Luther Abercrombie made his bow.

It was the first time the lawyer had defended anyone as definitely guilty as Rance Morgan, and the men of Kerr's Corners were anxious to see how the lawyer conducted himself. Some argued that Abercrombie couldn't lose; he had too many tricks in his bag.

"If he gits Morgan off this charge by legal tricks we'll lynch the both of 'em," promised one of the more sincere townsmen.

There were others who said that Abercrombie wouldn't dare to contend that Morgan was innocent of murder, but that the lawyer hoped to win a verdict of life imprisonment for his client.

Abercrombie conducted himself in a manner that satisfied everyone. He maintained a formal dignity that flattered, and completely won over, the judge on the bench; he referred to Bat Kester, the chief witness against Rance Morgan, as "the state's witness," or as "Mister Kester"; he asked questions in a simple and direct manner and accepted the answers without argument.

Abercrombie made no comments or objections while the case for the state was being presented. He treated everyone with the utmost respect and, aside from a few who were determinedly suspicious, made a highly favorable impression on the spectators.

In fact, it was Rance Morgan himself who gave the spectators most reason for suspicion. Although the web was being drawn closer and closer about him, he sat unmoved and unconcerned, and showed no sign of anger or resentment at the things that were said. Not once did he look at Bat Kester with the glance of hatred that was so well known and dreaded.

Kester, nervous at first, became completely at ease on the witness stand when Rance Morgan smiled quite openly.

This conduct on the part of a man who was on trial for murder kept suspense at a high pitch. Everyone expected that any moment might see the lawyer toss a bombshell into the proceedings that would throw a brand-new light upon the case and set his client free.

Yet nothing of the sort happened. There was no attempt to discredit what Bat Kester or anyone else had to say; there was no plea for Morgan on the ground that he had killed in self-defense. Abercrombie didn't even try to claim that Morgan was justified in committing murder. When it was brought out that the murder had not only been premeditated, but had been done purely for profit and in a cruel, ruthless manner, Abercrombie tacitly agreed by keeping silent.

It was inevitable that the verdict would be "Guilty."

The foreman of the jury read the verdict it had reached with less than ten minutes deliberation. It was then Luther Abercrombie rose impressively and cleared his throat.

A wave rustled through the crowd as everyone leaned forward in his seat. "Now it's comin'," muttered several men at once.

"Your honor," began the tall, lean lawyer. "It has been found that my client is guilty of murder as charged in the indictment. May I have a word before you pass sentence on him?"

Judge Phineas Jones, smugly pleased with himself and assuming full credit for the smooth progression of the trial, nodded quickly and beamed upon the suave attorney.

"We all know," said Abercrombie with dramatic pauses that built up intense interest in every word, "that the logical, the reasonable, in fact the proper thing to do when a man is found guilty of foul and ruthless murder, is to hang him."

If anyone but Abercrombie had been speaking there would have followed a chorus of shouted agreement to this statement. Abercrombie heard no interruption. The crowd hung on his every word.

"This case might be looked upon as typical of wanton slaughter. I have defended Rance Morgan because a man in my profession is like a doctor, he must serve humanity to the best of his ability. I have done my utmost to assure the prisoner a trial that was fair and not tainted by any condemnation of public opinion. I have seen to it that the jury has considered its decision on the strength of the facts as presented in this court and not on hearsay or personal feelings."

Phineas Jones interrupted. "Mister Abercrombie," said His Honor, "you ain't runnin' fer office so nevermine the fancy talk. Say what you got tuh say an' let's get on with the hangin'."

Luther Abercrombie frowned and pursed his lips to show that he felt offended. He bowed to the judge and said, "I will get on with the point I was about to make."

The packed assemblage shifted to more comfortable positions while the speaker cleared his throat and wiped his broad brow with a square of beautifully white linen which he tucked back in the pocket of his coat.

"When the defendant is hanged and dies," he said, "he will carry everything that he knows to his grave with him." He pointed dramatically at Rance Morgan.

"Inside that killer's brain lie facts that would wipe out every criminal within the confines of our county. As long as that man lives, there is a chance that he will repent of his sins and seek to make peace with his Creator by seeking to right some of his great wrongs."

He launched into a lengthy and dramatic effort to show how the worst of criminals had seen the error of their ways. He quoted many, many cases all of which, he claimed, were known to him personally where confessions had been signed by prisoners and innumerable criminals brought to justice. Several of the men who watched and listened squirmed in their seats at the prospect of Rance Morgan turning "squealer."

"Just as the state's witness made it possible for the conviction of Rance Morgan, so Rance Morgan might make possible the capture and conviction of every man who has aided him in his past criminal existence."

He concluded with an impassioned plea to keep the man alive, to refrain from hanging him and thus ruin all chance of bringing additional criminals to justice.

Luther Abercrombie made a splendid speech. The judge listened to it, every word of it, and waited until the lawyer had completely finished. He even gave him the chance to go on when he said, "You got anything more tuh add tuh that, Mister Abercrombie?"

"No," said the thin man. "I have nothing more to say."

Phineas bobbed his bald head. "All right then. The prisoner will stand an' face the court."

Rance Morgan stood.

"I sentence you," said the judge, "tuh be taken tuh the jail an' held there . . ."

Morgan grinned.

The judge continued. ". . . held there until sunrise

tomorrow mornin' at which time you'll be taken by the sheriff or by men designated by him an' hanged by the neck until you are dead."

Rance Morgan's face went livid and he bellowed a mighty cry of blackest rage. The crowd roared agreement. No one heard the last words of the judge, "And may God have mercy on your soul."

The trial satisfied everyone. Everyone, that is, excepting Morgan and Bat Kester. Morgan's words rang in Bat Kester's ears to haunt him for many hours to come. The threats, the vows, the promises were that he, Morgan, would get square if he had to come back from his grave to do it.

While men slapped one another on the back and agreed that the trial was a humdinger all the way through, Phineas Jones sought out Luther Abercrombie.

"I'm downright sorry about the verdict," the judge said. "You gave one o' the slickest speeches I ever heard in any court an' I was watchin' the crowd while you was doin' it. If the crowd had showed that they agreed with you, by noddin' heads while you was goin' at it, I'd of put Morgan in the calaboose fer life."

"I understand," said Abercrombie.

"The crowd wasn't with you, Abercrombie. They was lookin' dark an' I knowed that if I didn't dish up the death penalty there would be a lynchin' as sure as thunder."

Abercrombie said, "I knew while I was speaking that

it was quite useless. You *had* to sentence Rance Morgan to be hanged."

The lawyer walked away adding another comment for himself alone, "In fact, I counted on it. It will mean at least ten thousand dollars more from Rance Morgan."

CHAPTER VII

A MAN HANGS

Jim Peabody was determined to take no chances. By the time Rance Morgan was brought back to his cell from the courthouse, the lawman had sworn in extra deputies, and was prepared to maintain a four-man guard at all hours of the day and night until the execution had taken place.

The sheriff felt that friends of Morgan might have decided to wait until after the trial before making any attempt to take their leader out of custody. Everyone in town, in fact, expected a jail break. Tension increased with every hour that passed.

Luther Abercrombie went from the courthouse to his office, pausing frequently on the way to shake the hands of his admirers and accept congratulations on the manner in which he had conducted himself.

Morgan, the prisoner, subsided sullenly after his outburst in court. He reminded the sheriff of a smouldering volcano, likely to erupt at any instant.

One man walked alone from the courthouse without pausing to speak to anyone. His heels, contrary to the mode of the place, were flat and low. He appeared no taller than the average man in town and no attention was given him. Had he worn the style of boots that were most familiar, he would have towered head and shoulders above the average man, especially if he had stood erect. The Lone Ranger's slouching posture was awkward for him, but it was an essential part of his disguise. He wanted to attract as little attention as possible.

At a corner of the town the stranger paused and waited. In a few moments Tonto joined him.

"Listen carefully, Tonto," the Lone Ranger said softly. "I'm going back to camp now. You'll have to stay here and keep a sharp lookout. I've an idea that things will happen between now and sunrise tomorrow morning."

"That right."

"Rance Morgan seemed to be very much surprised when he heard the hanging sentence. I wonder if that lawyer double-crossed him?"

"Tonto not know," said the Indian.

"If that's the case, we'll hear from Morgan's men." Tonto nodded.

The Lone Ranger was about to speak but something won his attention. For some time he stood gazing silently toward the jail where guards were pacing with loaded rifles on their shoulders.

"Where did the sheriff get all those deputies?" he asked at last.

"Those all feller from town."

"Are you sure they're townsmen?"

"Tonto sure."

The Lone Ranger said, "Tonto, those men may be

townsmen, but they certainly aren't the sheriff's best men. Maybe he doesn't know that at least two of them served jail sentences in Los Santos county. Is it possible that Peabody himself is playing into the hands of Rance Morgan?"

Tonto shook his head slowly. "Not if him know it," he declared positively.

"The sheriff impressed me as being a pretty honest sort of man," the Lone Ranger agreed.

"Him on level," said the Indian flatly.

"That's more than I can say for some of those deputies."

For a moment longer, the two men discussed the situation. The Lone Ranger declared he had strong doubts that a jail break would be attempted before nightfall. In the meantime he would go to the camp, pack their duffel, and then return to town after dark to take up the watch with Tonto.

"If nothing happens," the Lone Ranger said, "we'll be on hand for the hanging in the morning. However, if there is a jail break, we'll try a scheme of our own."

"What do-um?" queried Tonto.

"If Morgan's friends take him out of jail they'll figure on being chased. They'll be prepared to outrun or outfight any posse that can be quickly organized to go after them, and then head for one of their regular hiding places. We'll let them lead us right to that hiding place. Then we can plan how to corral them there."

As the Lone Ranger left his Indian friend, Luther

Abercrombie strode to the sheriff's office and stated that he wanted to see his client.

"I dunno as there's any use you seein' him now," said Sheriff Peabody. "You done all you can do for him."

"Perhaps I can persuade Rance Morgan to divulge some of his secrets and prepare to meet his Maker with a clear conscience."

"I doubt that like everything," grumbled Jim Peabody. "I asked Morgan if he wanted the preacher, but he said he didn't want nobody but Bat Kester."

"Is that so?"

"Yep. I seen men that was bein' et up inside because they was mad at someone, but never in my life have I seen a man as bound an' determined tuh kill another as Rance Morgan is tuh git Bat Kester. If Morgan wasn't due tuh hang right soon, I wouldn't give two cents fer Kester's life."

"You'd better let me see him then," said Luther Abercrombie.

"Sure, you can see him all you want," replied Jim Peabody agreeably. "I don't care how much you or anyone else looks at him, but by thunder I ain't takin' a chance. Not even a little chance. Before you go tuh talk tuh him, I'm goin' to search you."

Abercrombie smiled in his tight-lipped manner and said, "Go right ahead."

Jim Peabody ran his expert fingers over the lawyer's clothing, patting all his pockets for a gun or knife but found no weapon of any kind. "You'd have a fine chance hidin' one," he commented, "by ginger, you're so thin, Mister Abercrombie, you can't even hide yore ribs."

The other frowned at this comment on his physique and then walked through the door the sheriff opened and sat down on the bunk next to Rance Morgan.

The sheriff couldn't hear a word that was said in spite of his attempts to do so.

Lawyer and client conducted their conference in the faintest of whispers. At first, Abercrombie did the talking. Jim Peabody could see the tense look in Rance Morgan's face relax. Then Morgan put his mouth close to the lawyer's ear and spoke while Abercrombie nodded. When the interview ended, half an hour later, the prisoner was an entirely different man.

As darkness fell upon Kerr's Corners the street became crowded with people. Everyone who was old enough to pack a gun was on hand. Each man felt sure an attempt would be made to take the prisoner out of jail. Everyone suspected his neighbor, or the man who stood nearest to him, of being one of the secret army of the condemned man.

The air of friendship that generally prevailed in western towns was missing. Everyone was glum and silent, but nevertheless on hand and ready for a fight.

The hours dragged slowly, but the passing of time brought no let down in the vigilance.

Guards paced on all four sides of the building that housed the prisoner. Additional guards slept on the floor in Jim Peabody's office. Unless the majority of the men in town were in Rance Morgan's gang, there wasn't the slightest chance of getting the captive out of jail alive.

Just before the first light of dawn a tremor of expectancy passed through Kerr's Corners. The moon had gone and no light came from the stars. It was the darkest part of the night. Now if ever, the jail break would be attempted. But nothing happened.

As daylight came men could not credit their senses. It wasn't reasonable for this hanging to proceed without a hitch. It didn't seem possible for a man of Rance Morgan's type, with the wide circle of criminal friends he must have, to go to this death with nothing more exciting than anticipation of action. Yet that seemed to be the case.

Morgan came from his cell heavily tied and guarded by six men with rifles. He was placed upon an unsaddled horse and headed toward a special grim-shaped tree outside the town. Jim Peabody had gone on ahead because he had to walk. Morgan rode with a guard on each side, two guards in front, and two more bringing up the rear.

It was a grim and determined group that headed for the hangman's tree.

The coroner, who was also the town's doctor, drove his own buckboard and took along Luther Abercrombie, dignified in a stovepipe hat, as his passenger.

Under the gallows tree Rance Morgan sat on the bare back of a horse and looked about him. His eyes were sharp and piercing as he studied first one, then another of the witnesses. Each time he saw a member of the jury that had found him guilty he stared in a fashion that made the man squirm uneasily.

Jim Peabody stepped forward. "Have you anything you want to say before we carry out the Judge's sentence?" he asked.

Rance Morgan rumbled, "Where's Bat Kester?"

"In jail. I left orders for him to be moved to the reg'lar jail as soon as you were taken out o' there. Why?"

"You can give him a message fer me."

"Sure thing, Morgan."

"Tell Kester that he knows what I said before. I told the polecat that if he squealed I'd get him for it. I'm a man that keeps his word. I will get him. I'll get him in a way that'll make what's about to happen to me seem like a picnic!"

"All right, Morgan," replied the sheriff in a soft voice. "I'll tell him what you said."

As the deputies were adjusting the noose about Rance Morgan's neck, the condemned man lifted his voice and addressed the crowd.

"I know what all of you are thinkin'," he roared. "You smile when I promise tuh come back from where I'm going an' get square. Well, you won't be smilin' when you go to bed tonight. You'll realize then that I ain't loco. I *know* what I'm talkin' about. I'll get square for this an' from that time on there won't be a human alive that will be able to get me! Now before I go, I'll tell you what I think of you."

Morgan's long, pent-up fury broke loose in a wave of condemnation that made strong men grow pale. He vowed terrible punishment for those who had decided that he should hang. He voiced grim threats with a sincerity that made those who heard him wonder if death, when it came, could put an end to the leader of the outlaw band.

Morgan was speaking his loudest when Jim Peabody could stand no more. The big sheriff raised his hand and signaled.

There was silence for several moments. A moment later the coroner stepped back and said, "I pronounce this man dead."

Murmurs from the crowd. A sigh of relief, but no cheers at the killer's end.

Rance Morgan's body was placed in a mule-drawn wagon while the spectators rode slowly back to Kerr's Corners.

Luther Abercrombie smiled upon the coroner and said, "Now we can return."

"I wonder," replied the driver of the buckboard, "how Bat Kester'll take this?"

"I wonder," Luther Abercrombie mused. "I wonder."

CHAPTER VIII

THE LONE RANGER RIDES

Croyden's Gulch went nowhere. It was a gash that had been cut into a sort of plateau by a river that had long since dried up. If the canyon had been a short cut for the people who lived in Kerr's Corners it might have been cleared out and used as a trail, but this was not the case. It had been neglected for so many generations that the weeds and brush that found rich nourishment in the soft, black loam of the old river bottom flourished until passage was almost an impossibility.

Rance Morgan's grave was situated on a hillside less than a hundred yards from the entrance to the gulch. This was a fact that was given no consideration at the time, but one which later took on grim significance.

The men who buried Rance Morgan's pine coffin finished their task and gave the mound of soft earth a few final pats with the backs of their spades. They tossed their tools into the wagon that had brought the killer's remains to the place. Two men climbed to the wagon seat, while the rest mounted their horses, and the whole party headed for the town.

The Lone Ranger stood at the edge of the woods watching the scene on the distant hill, but there was a look of disinterest in his face. He was still dressed in the dusty old clothes he had worn as a spectator at the trial and so far had said nothing to Tonto about his plans.

Tonto watched the Lone Ranger with anxiety. He had never before seen the white man look so discouraged.

The two stood there beside their horses for some time after the townsmen disappeared. Tonto waited the Lone Ranger's decision.

Finally the white man spoke. "I had hoped," he said, "to see the whole gang rounded up. I was sure something would happen that would give us some idea who the others were."

Tonto suggested that, with its leader gone, the gang might disband.

"There's no chance of that," replied the other shaking his head slowly. "Those men will select a new leader and the crimes that have terrorized everyone around here will continue as before."

The Lone Ranger and Tonto mounted slowly and headed into the woods toward a clearing where some of their supplies had been left.

"There is much work ahead," the Lone Ranger said thoughtfully. "I know for a fact that Morgan has a big gang working for him, or *did* have. Yet I doubt if even the members of the gang know who the other members are."

"Mebbe Kester feller know."

The Lone Ranger shook his head. "No, Tonto. I

think the only man Kester knew anything about was Rance Morgan himself."

For several minutes the two rode silently. Tonto wanted desperately to offer some suggestion to his friend, but could think of nothing that would help them uncover the Morgan gang.

"You told me," said the Lone Ranger, "Morgan was quite at ease and not at all concerned when he was arrested?"

"That right," agreed the Indian quickly.

"When he was on trial I saw for myself how lightly he treated his arrest. Yet it seemed that his sentence came as a complete surprise to him."

Tonto nodded.

"When Morgan went to jail after the trial he was a badly frightened man. He was convinced that he was going to hang and that nothing could save him. That's why he was so desperately anxious to get square with Bat Kester. Then Luther Abercrombie called on him. The two talked for a little while and Morgan was once more at ease."

"What Abercrombie say?"

"That's what I'd like to know, Tonto. I've been trying to figure out what Abercrombie might have told Rance Morgan. He might have said that some of the gang would come to save him. He might have said that there were plans that would rescue him at the last minute."

The Lone Ranger lapsed into a long spell of silence

while he rode slowly through the trees. Then he looked at Tonto and saw the dejection in the Indian's face.

"We're not beaten yet," he said. "Cheer up, Tonto, there must be *some* way we can get at the rest of the Morgan gang."

Tonto shook his head. "Tonto not know-um how," he said softly. "Morgan gang plenty smart."

"Smart enough to keep quiet for a time? I doubt it. With Morgan gone they will have to select a new leader. Something may happen."

The Lone Ranger knew the type of men that comprised the Morgan gang, even though he didn't know who those men were. Desperate, ruthless, utterly bad in every way, they stopped at nothing, and were known even to have committed murder to prevent identification. Though they moved among their fellowmen in town, carrying out commonplace pursuits, they remained desperadoes at heart. Surely there would be fierce rivalry in the choosing of a leader to supplant Rance Morgan.

Even if the Lone Ranger's surmise was correct there was nothing he could do. He chafed at the thought of sitting back and waiting. Besides, no matter what happened, the capture of the entire gang at one time was too much to hope. Yet, as long as there was a single survivor, the Lone Ranger could not rest.

The two horses arrived at a clearing in the woods.

Tonto dismounted and rolled back a log. It was beneath this log, in a hole that was covered by protecting tarpaulin, that the Indian had left the extra clothing and supplies. Now he brought these into the open and examined them while he waited for the Lone Ranger to reach some sort of decision.

The Lone Ranger sat on the ground beside a pool of clear water, thinking, while he pulled the disguise of false hair from his eyebrows and clean-shaved upper lip.

"There must be some key to this thing," he muttered.

Tonto looked up quickly—hopefully. From past experience the Indian knew that when his friend began to mutter his thoughts in that concentrated way, a plan of action was forming in the Lone Ranger's mind.

"Abercrombie talked with Rance Morgan and the killer's spirits were lifted. Something he said made Morgan feel that he would not hang. What *could* have been said?"

The Lone Ranger was putting facts together, trying to arrive at some conclusion that might form the basis for an attack that would carry the battle for justice into the heart of the enemy camp.

"Perhaps the lawyer told Rance Morgan that he would be rescued by his gang. No! Morgan would know that Abercrombie wasn't telling the truth unless —*unless* Abercrombie knew the men in Morgan's gang."

The Lone Ranger stopped speaking suddenly. He rose to his feet and looked at Tonto. In his eyes there was a new light. Tonto crouched tensely, watching the tall man.

"Tonto!" barked the Lone Ranger. "The key man in this thing is Abercrombie himself!"

An expression of disappointment showed on the face of the Indian.

"Well, why not?" demanded the Lone Ranger.

"Him," said Tonto, "plenty good friend of law."

"A friend of the sheriff?"

Tonto nodded.

"That doesn't mean a thing! He might easily pose as a friend of Sheriff Peabody and still know Rance Morgan's men. Morgan trusted Abercrombie with his *life,* didn't he? Isn't it likely that he'd be willing to trust him with everything?"

The Indian looked dubious, but said that he was ready to follow any suggestion.

The Lone Ranger's plan developed rapidly once it was started. He pulled off the dusty, patched shirt he'd been wearing and tossed it, with his limp-brimmed hat, to Tonto.

"Better get these old clothes stowed away and my regular outfit unpacked," he said as he dropped to his knees beside the pool. He soused his face and neck with water, scrubbing vigorously to remove all traces of the stain and spirit gum for the false hair that had made up his disguise.

While he dried his face and hands, the Lone Ranger said, "I'll need my own guns and the belts of cartridges. Be sure those guns are loaded with the silver bullets.

The mask too, Tonto, get that ready." The ruddy glow of perfect health came to the clean-cut face of the Lone Ranger as he finished with the towel.

Tonto caught something of the electric enthusiasm of the white man. He moved quickly about the clearing fetching guns and bullets. He brought forth the Lone Ranger's high-heeled boots and rubbed them to a high luster.

"No need for you to do that," the Lone Ranger said. "I can keep my own boots shined."

Tonto grinned. "Me like," he said.

The Indian, even though he knew but little of what the Lone Ranger had in mind, was delighted to see his good hearty spirits return.

The old low-heeled boots were yanked off and tossed aside and then the faded, blue denim dungarees. In place of them the white man climbed into clean black trousers that fitted closely to his calves and thighs and made it easier to ride and fight. He hauled on his boots and then stuck his arms into a shirt that was the color of soft buckskin. A neckerchief and hat completed his dressing. He strapped on his cartridge belts and guns, checking the guns to make sure they were ready for action. Last of all, he fastened a mask across his eyes and tied it behind his head.

Once again the Lone Ranger looked his familiar self. He was erect, in contrast to his former slumping posture. Naturally tall, he was made even taller by the high heels of his boots. His mouth and chin showed a fixed determination, and his eyes, gleaming through the slits of the mask, were deep and steely.

"Now," the masked man said, "we're ready."

While the Lone Ranger had been strapping on his belts and mask, Tonto had stowed the discarded clothing in saddlebags and blanket rolls. He stood beside the paint horse ready to follow the masked man.

"Where," said Tonto, "we go-um? What do now?"

"We're going to Kerr's Corners and I'll tell you what we're going to do while we're riding."

Tonto nodded and leaped for the saddle.

The weight of the Lone Ranger's left foot on the stirrup was all that Silver needed. The big white stallion, as eager as the masked man to be in action, was under way before the rider hit the saddle.

"Hi-Yo," the masked man cried. "Hi-Yo, Silver, Away-y-y-y."

The shout was hardly needed. Silver was already traveling fast, dodging among the trees of the woods in the general direction of Kerr's Corners.

CHAPTER IX

AT THE GULCH'S MOUTH

"Hi-Yo, Silver, Away-y-y!" The cry of the Lone Ranger rang out on the plain between the woods and the town. A few who were in the street at Kerr's Corners heard the distant shout and looked. They saw a white form streaking ahead of a cloud of dust, heading toward the community like a comet.

As the masked rider came nearer, those who watched saw that partly hidden by the dust there was a second horse and rider.

Silver raced into town, his hard, sharp hoofs pounding until the earth itself seemed to shake and tremble. People standing near the buildings stared at the hard-riding men; they saw a flash and then found themselves showered by dust that filled their eyes and nostrils.

"What a horse!" cried one man.

Loud yells came from others. Someone shouted, "I heard him. I know who 'tis!"

Jim Peabody heard the thundering hoofs and looked out of his window as a silvery flame lanced by. He caught one brief glimpse of Tonto and bellowed in a way that brought the prisoner, Bat Kester, to his feet. "The Lone Ranger!"

Everyone in town was taken by complete surprise at

the startling entry of the masked man. The rider leaped to the ground in front of Luther Abercrombie's office.

"Watch 'em," he called to Tonto. "I'm going inside."

Without the formality of knocking on the lawyer's door, the masked man burst inside.

Tonto leaped to a position at the door and snatched two guns from his belt. He waited, watching intently for anyone who had ideas about entering the lawyer's office.

Deputy Sheriff Jack Tilson was the first to approach. "Stand aside," he cried. "I want tuh know what's goin' on here."

Tonto jerked his gun a bit in warning.

"You can't ride through here like you owned the place," threatened the deputy. "An' who's that masked man? What's he want with Mister Abercrombie?"

"You find out plenty soon," replied the Indian.

Other men came up and ranged beside the lawman. There were threats and shouts of rage. "What are these fellas up tuh? Arrest the two of 'em. What's bein' done tuh Mister Abercrombie? Come on, boys, toss that redskin tuh one side an' we'll go get that masked hombre."

Tonto stood silently, his guns held steady while he darted quick glances from one to another of the men who were shouting.

Mike Turner, the most recent of the deputy sheriffs appointed by Jim Peabody, came up at that point and asked, "What're you scairt of?"

"Careful, Mike," warned Jack Tilson. "That redskin

means business with them six-shooters of his. Don't take any chances."

"I never yet seen a redskin that dared throw a gun on *me*," retorted Mike Turner. "I'm takin' those shootin' irons away from him."

He raised his voice. "Yuh hear me, Injun? I'm comin' for yuh, an' if you make a move tuh shoot, there'll be a dozen lead slugs in yuh so quick you won't know what struck yuh."

Mike Turner reached for his gun. There was a sudden shot, a lance of flame from one of Tonto's guns.

A dozen pairs of eyes swung toward Mike Turner. The deputy's face showed wide-eyed amazement while he wiped his gun hand across the front of his shirt. The gun, which had been half drawn from the holster, lay on the ground ten feet away. It was ruined beyond repair by Tonto's well-directed shot.

Turner's hand was not struck by the bullet, but it stung from the force of the blow on his gun. Jack Tilson said, "I told yuh tuh be careful."

There was no further attempt on anyone's part to draw a gun.

A new commotion caught the crowd's attention. A yell and then a scream came from inside the lawyer's office.

"No-no-no," cried the voice of Luther Abercrombie. "Don't take me away."

The Lone Ranger appeared in the doorway. He had Abercrombie, whose hands were tied, slung over one shoulder like a sack of flour. He supported the lawyer with one hand while he held a gun in the other.

"Good work, Tonto. Keep them covered until I mount my horse; then I'll watch them until you're mounted."

"I'm givin' yuh fair warnin'," shouted Mike Turner who apparently hadn't learned that his boasts and threats meant little to the determined pair. "You abduct that man an' we'll hunt yuh down an' hang yuh if it's the last thing we do."

The Lone Ranger acted as if he had not heard the deputy. He tossed the squealing, kicking lawyer across Silver's back and swung into the saddle.

"Stand right where you are. All of you," he ordered. "Get mounted, Tonto."

Tonto leaped from the porch to the saddle without touching foot to either the ground or the stirrup. Abercrombie's yells of fear were drowned by the pounding of hoofs. A dust cloud swirled about the spectators who stared in disbelief at the bold abduction in broad daylight. The Lone Ranger and Tonto were gone, and Luther Abercrombie was gone with them.

The Lone Ranger raced across the plains once more, but this time instead of cutting to his left and heading for the woods he struck toward the entrance to Croyden's Gulch.

Half an hour of riding brought the masked man and his prisoner to the gulch where Silver was drawn to a halt.

Abercrombie, lowered to the ground, sank in sheer exhaustion from the wild ride on the mighty horse.

Tonto leaped beside the fallen man and looked him over carefully.

"I hope that ride wasn't too much for him," the masked man said.

After a pause Tonto said, "Him all right." He took a canteen from beside the saddle of his horse and poured water on the lawyer's face.

Abercrombie sputtered, then moaned and opened his eyes. He was a sorry-looking spectacle. The black suit he wore was hardly suitable for the ride he had had, it was covered with dust and badly wrinkled. His formerly crisp white shirt was limp and bedraggled, and his tie and collar were gone—pulled off in the struggle.

"Th-there's a law against this kind of thing," said Luther Abercrombie when he felt strong enough to speak. "You can't abduct a man in this fashion. I'll drag you through every court in the land, if necessary, and make you pay and pay plenty for what you've done to me."

"Before you talk about courts," replied the masked man calmly, "you'd better look around and get your bearings. Right behind you is Croyden's Gulch."

Abercrombie turned and looked. Quickly his small sharp eyes turned to meet the steely ones behind the mask.

"What about it?" he demanded.

"We're quite alone here. You'll find no help near by."

"We won't be alone for long. I have friends in town, plenty of them. They'll come here and kill you for this. You let me go and I'll do my best to get you off this abduction charge with a term in prison. Hold me here until my friends come and I promise you, you'll hang."

The Lone Ranger could not help but admire the spunk of the helpless and totally unarmed lawyer.

"Threats of that kind don't worry me," he said. "I've heard them too many times before."

"Why did you do this? What do you want?"

"I want to know all about Rance Morgan's gang."

Luther Abercrombie said, "I don't know anything about them."

"That's the answer I expected. That's why we came here."

"What's being here to do with it? I told you in my office, I know nothing."

"And," said the Lone Ranger, "I told you I didn't believe you. I still don't. For the last time, answer me."

"For the last time?"

"Yes. I'll not ask you again—now."

"I have nothing to say."

"Very well, then, Abercrombie, I'm going to leave you here to think it over. That's why we came here. No one ever goes into Croyden's Gulch. No one thinks it is possible to go there, and that's the last place anyone will search for you. Pick him up, Tonto."

The Indian picked the lawyer off the ground and

carried him deep into the dense brush in the gulch. There the Indian placed the lawyer on the ground and gagged him while the Lone Ranger looked on impassively.

"You may not be bothered much till after dark, Abercrombie, but when evening comes there are a lot of flies and insects and some of them sting quite badly. Perhaps you'll change your mind about—"

What the Lone Ranger was about to say was lost. A hard blow that came without warning struck him on the back of his head. It seemed as if a million stars erupted before his eyes. He felt himself groping in darkness, clutching with all his might for something to support him. Then he slumped to the ground.

Tonto rose from the ground to see why the Lone Ranger's speech was cut off so abruptly. He saw the masked man crumpling to the ground. Before the Indian could act a heavy gun exploded almost in his face. He had a fleeting impression of fire and smoke before it seemed as though his head was splitting, letting in an overwhelming wave of darkness.

Tonto fell across the bound form of Luther Abercrombie.

CHAPTER X

DEAD MAN'S RETURN

Jim Peabody fretted and grumbled while a posse rode in search of the abductors of Luther Albercrombie. He paced the floor of his office cursing the bulk that made it impossible to join the hunt. Whenever someone dropped in, the sheriff swung quickly toward the door with a look of expectancy. He turned an abrasive tongue loose on those who came to ask if there had been some word.

When the searchers finally returned it was late afternoon and the word they brought was anything but encouraging. To begin with, they'd found it difficult to follow the trail of the masked man's horse. When they reached hard-packed ground they had been forced to dismount and search tirelessly for the faint hoofmarks of the great white horse.

The trail finally led to Croyden's Gulch and there it stopped.

"Stopped?" roared Jim Peabody, "what d'yuh mean it stopped?"

"That's all there is tuh it," said Jack Tilson. "Me an' Mike Turner seen where the trail stopped about ten feet from the mouth of the gulch. I tell you, boss, it was downright mysterious. I never seen anything like it before."

Mike Turner verified what Tilson said. "What's more," he added, "nothin' went intuh the gulch."

"How do you know?" demanded the sheriff.

"We'd o' noticed the bent-down brushwood if anyone had gone in there."

"That's right," said Tilson. "There wasn't so much as a bent twig. You know what the entrance to Croyden's Gulch is like, Sheriff."

"I ain't seen it in years."

"Wal, it's the same as it was ten years ago, only more so. You can take our word for it."

Jim Peabody slumped into his chair. "Beat's all," he growled. "From the stories I've heard about this Lone Ranger, he's always on the right side. Now why in tarnation did he kidnap Mister Abercrombie?"

The deputies shook their heads.

"Where'd he go? Are you sure there wasn't no tracks leadin' away from where you claim the marks of the horses' hoofs stopped?"

"We're sure."

For several seconds the sheriff sat deep in thought. "Doggone!" he said irritably.

No one paid any attention to Bat Kester. The prisoner gripped the bars of his door with both hands and listened to all that was said.

The sheriff and his deputies discussed the strange disappearance of the three men and two horses for some time before the two deputies left. Jim Peabody sat alone, deep in thought.

Twilight came and went. Someone slipped into the office and lighted the oil lamps. Jim Peabody didn't notice. His wife came to see if he was coming home to eat. He didn't hear her. Bat Kester called out, "I'm gittin' hungry. When's grub comin' in?" Peabody made no sign that he had heard.

The sheriff had a peculiar feeling of impending trouble. It was something that had started with the hanging in the morning—a feeling that couldn't be accounted for, but one that persisted through the day with increasing intensity.

Rance Morgan had not acted as he should. The baffling manner of the condemned man was one thing that bothered the sheriff. The sudden appearance and subsequent disappearance of the Lone Ranger was another. What was coming next?

Far back in the lawmans mind was a tiny, isolated fact that he was trying to recall. He couldn't get at the fact, but he knew it was there. Something that dealt with Croyden's Gulch. Someone had said something about the place. Who was it that had told him? What was it that had been said? He felt that there was a connection between the vague item and the strange phenomenon of hoofmarks that faded into nothingness

Jim Peabody leaned forward on his desk, resting his chin in cupped hands. The deputies had reported that Rance Morgan's grave was near the gulch. That wasn't the item for which the sheriff probed his mind.There was something else about the gulch.

Dimly the sheriff heard a voice say, "Simon Buckley's dog." He jerked to attention.

"What's that?" snapped the sheriff.

It was Bat Kester who had spoken. "You remember," went on the prisoner from his cell. "Simon Buckley told about that big dog o' his."

And Jim Peabody did remember. In a flash the story came back to him. It dealt with Croyden's Gulch.

Simon Buckley was something of a character in town. He managed to eke out an uncertain existence by training dogs for hunting and herding and then selling them. When he had the chance to earn a bit of loose change, he did so by chopping wood or odd-jobbing. A few days ago, Simon Buckley came to town in a disconsolate mood. He had gone out hunting with his favorite dog, a big shaggy fellow with paws as big as the hoofs of a pony. The dog had flushed a bird at the entrance to Croyden's Gulch. Racing into the gulch the dog had let out a frightful cry of fear. It was not seen again.

Buckley had whistled and called without response. He had not ventured into the gulch because of the mass of growing things.

"Buckley's big dog," said Kester, "disappeared there."

"I remember," said the sheriff. "What I want tuh know, is *why!*"

"That doggoned gulch," muttered Kester with awe in his voice, "is hoodoo or somethin'. I'm hanged if I don't think the place is *haunted.*"

"Bah," snorted the big sheriff. "That's talk fer fools an' young 'uns."

"I don't know about that."

"Well, I do. I've heard a lot of darn fool superstitious notions from the loco cowpokes around here. There've been yarns of haunted canyons, haunted gold mines, haunted houses an' I dunno what else, but I never yet seen a thing o' that sort that didn't have a reasonable explanation. Trouble is in findin' that explanation."

Bat Kester shook his head. "I still ain't convinced," he said.

"Well, I'm goin' home. There's nothin' to hang around here for."

"You're givin' Abercrombie up fer dead?"

"Who says so," snapped the sheriff.

"Well, ain't yuh?"

"Not by a darn sight. I'll get more men out the first thing in the mornin'. If they come back with the same crazy story that Mike an' Jack have, by thunder, I'll get a wagon an' go see for myself."

Sheriff Peabody started for the door.

"Sheriff!"

"Well?" Peabody turned back toward his prisoner.

"I—I got somethin' I want tuh ask. You'll likely say I'm loco for even thinkin' such a thing, but I got tuh ask it anyway."

"Well, ask then!"

"I keep rememberin' what Morgan said. I mean about me."

"Rememberin' won't help your peace of mind. Forget it. Rance Morgan is dead an' buried."

"I—I can't forget it."

"Then remember it," barked the big lawman. "I got too much worry about men that're alive, at least I hope they're alive, tuh think about killers that've been executed for their crimes."

Bat Kester reached through the bars and grasped at Jim Peabody's shirt. "Don't leave me here alone," he begged. "Why don't you put a guard outside the jail. I—I don't want tuh be left alone."

"What the dickens are yuh scairt of?"

"I—I dunno." Bat Kester's face was drawn and his eyes were large with fear. "All I know is that Rance Morgan had a gang that was bigger'n any laws that was ever made. He often boasted as tuh how he'd never be killed fer keeps. He told me, an' I reckon he told the rest of his men, that if he was ever double-crossed, he'd come back from the dead, if he had tuh, tuh git square."

The sheriff was disgusted with the utterly hopeless fear of the prisoner. He spat on the floor. "That for what Rance Morgan said." He stalked to the door.

Jim Peabody paused at the door and studied the sky. It was overcast. "Rain 'fore mornin'," he mused. He saw his wife sitting on the porch across the road. Lights in the window behind her made her visible. He started down the steps of the office. It was then that he heard the yell from inside.

Bat Kester's voice carried a shrill, ear-splitting quality that comes only from men who face death and are afraid. The cry was choked off suddenly.

By the time Jim Peabody had wheeled, yanked open the door and plunged into the room, the only sound that came from Kester's cell was a gurgling choking noise. Even this stopped by the time the sheriff reached the barred door.

Peabody couldn't believe what he saw. The light in the cell fell across a small square window opposite the door. Close to the bars, pressing against them from outside, there was a man's face. Unbelievable as it was, the face was Rance Morgan's.

Hands outside the cell pulled hard on a rope. A noose in the rope was drawn taut about Bat Kester's neck. The prisoner's body slumped against the wall of the prison supported only by the rope.

A brief flash was all that Jim Peabody had of the weird scene before Morgan's face disappeared from the window. Bat Kester flopped to the floor with the noose still about his neck.

Peabody fumbled with his keys. He finally got the cell door open, but Kester was beyond all aid. The sound of horse's hoofs came from somewhere behind the jail, and faded away.

The sheriff wasted no time with Kester's body. He raced from the building shouting, ordering all who heard him to form a posse to pursue a man whose face looked like that of a man who had been twelve hours dead and ten hours buried.

Men came running from all directions. Some went back to get their horses while others snatched spare lanterns from the office, lighted them, and examined the ground outside the window.

"He must've been standin' right here," said Jim Peabody, pointing to the ground. "Lower a lantern here an' see if there ain't some footprints."

There were footprints. They were clear and unmistakable. Prints that showed where a man had stood while he tossed the noose through the bars of the window to strangle the man inside.

There also was a note. Several men recognized the writing as Rance Morgan's. It was signed with Morgan's name.

"I said I'd get him," the note stated, "and I've kept my word. You can't hang a man twice so I'm laughing at you. From now on, I'll tell what I want around here, and if I don't get it, I'll visit a few more folks that hated me."

"It ain't so," snarled the sheriff. "It can't be so! Someone wanted Kester dead an' tried to put the blame on a dead man. Rance Morgan didn't do this."

"It's his writin'," someone said.

"That don't mean a thing. His writin' could be copied."

There was some discussion on this point while Jack

Tilson gave the ground and the footprints a close scrutiny. "Here," the deputy said finally. "Take a look at this."

"A look at what?"

Tilson pointed to a particularly sharp footprint in the dirt. "Take a look at that," he said. "I remember Rance Morgan wearin' boots with a patch just like that."

"Me too," said another of the men.

"I'd know Morgan's footprints anywhere," chimed in a third while several others agreed.

Men of the West who lived the sort of lives that called for constant observation of minute details were keen-eyed. There wasn't the slightest doubt in the mind of anyone about the footprint.

The thing that made the mystery more baffling was the fact that a dozen men could swear the boots that made those telltale marks had been buried with the man who owned them.

The lengthy discussion was continued indoors when the storm broke. Jagged lightning and constant rumbling of thunder gave a weird background to the conference.

Several men came to add their voices to the tense conference. The doctor insisted that Rance Morgan's heart had stopped. Others were equally positive in their stories of his burial.

The talk lasted far into the night without a single satisfactory conclusion being reached. Rance Morgan *couldn't* have returned from the dead. Yet, in refutation of this, there was the note he'd left, his footprints, the sheriff's identification of his face at the window, and, most important of all, the fact that Bat Kester was dead.

CHAPTER XI

IN THE CAVE

Men whose eyes were still red-rimmed for lack of sleep sloshed through the muddy street of Kerr's Corners after an all night rain. Sheriff Jim Peabody had adjourned the meeting the night before until daybreak when there might be some hope of going after the murderer of Bat Kester.

Rain had probably washed out what tracks there might have been, but deputies like Tilson and Mike Turner were impatient at inaction, and argued that anything would be better than waiting idly in town for the possibility of another appearance by the man who had been hanged.

Then, too, Luther Abercrombie was still missing. The men who had formed the posse of the previous day were anxious to return to Croyden's Gulch and try again to penetrate the mystery of the tracks that disappeared. This time they were better equipped to search the gulch.

Axes and hatchets, knives and saws were loaded on a buckboard. Two strong horses were hitched in front and five men, all of them hand-picked by Jack Tilson for their courage and resourcefulness, swung to their saddles.

"I figure," Tilson told the sheriff, "that there's some

connection between all these things. It's just a hunch of mine, but I got the notion that if we can find out where that masked man went with the lawyer, we'll be in a fair way to findin' out how come Rance Morgan is a walkin' dead man."

Jim Peabody nodded. "I'd like tuh ride along with you men in that wagon."

"Of course, Sheriff, if yuh insist why it'll have tuh be all right with the rest of us," said Tilson. "But we aim tuh cut our way intuh the gulch an' it won't be easy goin'. We mayn't come back till sundown an' if we don't find what we're after, we'll camp near by an' start the hunt again tomorrow mornin'."

"I know, Tilson."

"It might be a sight better if you was to stay here an' keep the office runnin' in case somethin' else turns up."

"I reckon you're right."

Jack Tilson gave an order and, with his own horse hitched behind the rig, climbed to the seat and took the reins.

"Good luck tuh you," cried the sheriff.

The men called out to their horses and the group moved out of Kerr's Corners.

Jim Peabody stood in front of his office, watching until the small posse disappeared beyond a slight rise in the ground far out of the town. "Now," he mused, "we'll git somewhere. There should be news by sundown.

The Lone Ranger recovered consciousness slowly, his first awareness being a splitting pain that made his temples throb. He believed he was blind from the blow on his head. He tried to move, but found that his hands were lashed across his stomach. He lay flat on his back. He realized, too, that his feet were tied.

When he tried to turn, the effort sent a thousand pains stabbing through muscles that were cramped and strained. There was blackness around him. He blinked his eyes but saw nothing. He couldn't make out any object, not even the ground which was but six inches from his eyes.

As the Lone Ranger's mind grew a little clearer he rolled to feel with his hands the ground upon which he lay. It was cold and damp. It felt like earth with small stones scattered about.

He must have grunted slightly with the effort because a voice came from quite close at hand.

"You wake now?"

It was Tonto who spoke.

The Lone Ranger whispered, "Are you badly hurt?"

"Me get brush with bullet. Not hurt bad. Knock-um Tonto out."

"I can't see a thing."

"That right. Bad feller take us to cave."

"Where is the cave?"

"Me not know-um that."

"How long have we been here?"

Tonto replied that he knew very little. He had recovered consciousness long before the white man. He had seen vague light beyond the opening of a cavern before the storm arose. He, too, was bound and helpless. He told about the storm which had lasted most of the night and how the intermittent flares of lightning had shown him trees bending to the wind beyond the entrance of the cave. The storm had passed and left only silence, darkness.

"We were captured by someone," the Lone Ranger said as he tried to recall the last things before the blow that felled him. "You were tying Luther Abercrombie. Do you remember that?"

"Tonto remember. Me hear you stop talk. Me look. See gun flash, nothing more."

The discussion was carried on in whispers, but even these echoed hollowly in the cave. Tonto judged it must be almost dawn.

"I wonder if they took off my mask?"

Tonto said, "No." The Indian had caught a glimpse of the mask when lightning flashed an hour before.

"Is there any chance of getting your ropes loose?"

"Me try plenty long time. Rope plenty tight."

"That's my trouble. If my head will stop spinning I can put a little more effort into trying to get my hands free."

"You rest for time. We keep quiet till dawn. Then mebbe take-um look outside."

An early morning mist delayed the dawn, but even so it came sooner than either of the prisoners expected.

It broke gray tinged with purple beyond the mouth of the cave. By the time the first rays of the sun slanted down to evaporate the haze, the Lone Ranger felt much better.

His muscles were still cramped as before, but his headache had become more tolerable. It still pained him, and the throbbing persisted in his temples, but he could move without the giddiness which had threatened to rob him of consciousness.

Though the masked man and Tonto were tied about the wrists and ankles, they were able to squirm along the ground. Pebbles dug into their sides and stomachs as they snaked toward the entrance of their prison. The view, when they reached the goal, was worth the cost. They looked upon a tangle that might have been a jungle in the darkest part of Africa. The growth of weeds and ferns was luxuriant, almost tropical. Mist curled up from the damp mass of green as the sun's heat started a drying process.

Dragonflies and darning needles lanced about with myriads of other insects, catching the sun and reflecting it from the gaudy colors of their metallic-looking bodies. The cloying sweetness of the blossoms that tempted the flashing bits of life was mingled with a damp, rotting smell of decaying vegetation.

In all directions the view was cut off by the rank growth, but there could be no doubt about the cave's location. Nowhere, save in Croyden's Gulch, could nature have thrived so unmolested.

Tonto seemed more interested in the sun than in the growing things. He studied it through squinting eyes and wore a look of calculation as he did so.

"Mebbe," the Indian said at length, "sun be good friend."

"What do you mean by that, Tonto?"

"Mebbe sun get us free of rope."

Tonto had a plan of his own. Fifteen minutes later he began a series of deft movements that would have been a challenge to a contortionist. He squirmed about the ground, straining his chafed wrists against the ropes until the pain must have been intense.

He drew his hands first to one side, then to the other, stretching the rope the tiniest bit.

Tonto's hands were white from cut-off circulation. His fingers were heavy and clumsy, but he kept straining and fighting the restriction of the cords until one hand could reach a pocket in his buckskin jacket.

The Lone Ranger saw the Indian's fingers dip into the pocket, fumble for a moment, and then come out with a small round object that reflected the light.

The masked man saw now what Tonto had in mind. The object he held was the lens from an old pair of field glasses.

Tonto grinned as he saw the expression on the masked man's face. "Now," he said, "we get loose plenty soon."

The Lone Ranger knew what was expected of him. He turned so Tonto could hold the optical glass between the sun and the ropes. A white light, brighter than the sun itself, fell on the masked man's wrists.

Tonto adjusted the position of the glass until the light was concentrated in a tiny pin point. It struck the Lone Ranger's wrists and burned. The masked man moved his hands to bring the ropes beneath the concentration of the sun's heat. A wisp of smoke threaded from the ropes where a brown, charred spot appeared as if by magic. Several of the strands burned through.

The masked man moved to bring the heat rays on another portion of the hemp. Bit by bit, the strands were burned until a final jerk snapped the remaining cords. It required but a few moments then to free Tonto's hands, and for each man to untie his own feet.

The next few moments were spent in massaging arms and legs, in limbering up muscles that had been cruelly strained, before the two inspected each other's wounds. Tonto's was superficial. The bullet had just grazed his scalp. Fortunately for the masked man, his hat had saved him from serious injury. Without that padding, the blow he had sustained might easily have fractured his skull.

Next the men took inventory of their position. They were without their guns. Their horses, of course, were missing.

"The first thing to do," decided the Lone Ranger, "is to round up our horses. We'll get out of this gulch, and see what we can find around the entrance where we were attacked."

Tonto agreed.

"After that, we'll have a look around for Luther Abercrombie. I'm more than ever convinced that, if he wants to, he can tell a lot that will be of importance."

"Me want to find feller who shoot."

"Did you get a look at him?"

"Not get-um chance."

"No idea who he was?"

Tonto shook his head.

"At any rate, we've learned that Croyden's Gulch is *not* impassable. We were brought in here, and if we were brought in, others could come in. I want to know more about this place, *lots* more about it."

"Wait." Tonto's voice was soft and tense. He reached out and gripped the masked man's arm. "Someone come this way."

The Lone Ranger's first impulse was to leap out and confront the men who approached; just in time, he remembered that he was unarmed. With Tonto he drew back to the furthermost part of the cave.

A moment later two men appeared and paused in the sunlight at the cavern's mouth. They were familiar figures, both of them. Broad daylight left no room for doubt as to their identity. The masked man was at first inclined to mistrust his senses, to think his eyes were playing tricks on him.

But there could be no doubt—the larger of the men outside was Rance Morgan! The other was the lawyer Luther Abercrombie!

"I'll go inside," Rance Morgan was saying, "I'll get the extra cash you've got comin', an' while I'm there I'll see about the prisoners."

"I'd like to get a chance at them," shrilled Abercrombie in his high-pitched voice. "Why not let me finish them off, if you don't want to do it."

"You think I'm holding back because I'm afraid tuh kill 'em? Don't take me for a fool, Abercrombie. When I think the time is right I'll let 'em have it, an' it'll be done in a way that'll be anything but pleasant. First of all, there are a few things I want tuh find out about 'em, an' the best way tuh do that will be tuh keep 'em alive."

"Hurry then, I'll wait out here."

"I will."

"Oh, another thing," said Abercrombie as Morgan started into the cave.

Morgan turned. "Well?"

"While you're getting the cash, remember that we owe a tidy sum of money to the doctor who pronounced you dead and to the rest of the boys who let you slip out of the coffin."

"They're all my own men. They'll get their cut on cash when we have our regular split up."

"Well, remember, we promised five hundred dollars to Jack Tilson for fixing a rope around your chest beneath your shirt so they could make believe to hang you."

"I've already dealt with Tilson. He and some of the

rest of the boys are coming here this afternoon. Maybe this morning. They'll disappear and then when you tell your story around in town, this gulch will be a downright mysterious place that folks'll stay away from."

"Very well," replied the lawyer. "You're still the boss of the gang."

The Lone Ranger had never in his life heard of such a far-flung, widespread, well-organized gang of out-laws. It appeared that practically everyone of any official position in town was a member of the gang. The doctor, the sheriff's deputies, the lawyer. No one knew how many more! He had some of the information that he had abducted the lawyer to secure, but how could he use it? If he simply told what he knew no one would believe him. He must find some means of exposing the gang to the townspeople.

Rance Morgan entered the cave.

CHAPTER XII

DEFEAT AND DESPAIR

It took but a moment for Rance Morgan to realize that his prisoners had gotten loose. With the discovery, he let out a sharp gasp of surprise and with incredible speed ducked out the mouth of the cave.

The Lone Ranger was about to leap after the man in the hope of capturing him, but Tonto held him back with a firm grip on his arm.

Morgan didn't pause. Catching the lawyer by one arm, he fairly dragged Abercrombie the way they had come. Morgan shouted the story of his discovery while the two raced on their way.

When the masked man and Tonto left the cave, they did so softly and with extreme caution. Tonto's better judgment had prevailed in this instance. The two were at the mercy of anyone who held a gun, and further handicapped by a lack of knowledge of the gulch. The better course for the moment was to follow Morgan and his partner-in-crime and see where they went.

Tonto led the way, dodging along between the tangle of green things without making a sound. Following in the Indian's footsteps, the Lone Ranger, too, moved noiselessly. Ahead, they could hear the plotters even though they couldn't see them.

For the better part of half an hour the Lone Ranger and Tonto pushed on through the gulch. For the past five minutes they hadn't been able to hear the steps of the men ahead, but they knew that Abercrombie and Rance Morgan must be there.

The sides of the canyon were close together, too close for Tonto to have passed the men ahead; also, the sides were too steep. There was only one way for the crooks to travel and that way led to the gulch's opening.

As he moved along, the Lone Ranger recalled that apparently there was a supply of money in the cave. The place must have been the hide-out for the loot of the Morgan gang. The cave might hold many secrets that could be investigated at a later time. The present need was guns and horses.

Unexpectedly Tonto broke from cover to an open plain with the Lone Ranger right behind him. They had left the gulch to find themselves at the spot where they'd been struck down the night before. They could see for miles in all directions, but there wasn't the slightest sign of Rance Morgan or Luther Abercrombie.

More baffling than the disappearance of the men, was the lack of footprints on the ground. Rain had turned the hard dirt soft and spongy, a perfect surface for a mark of any kind. The tracks of the Lone Ranger and Tonto as they stepped from the gulch were clearly visible. Yet there was no sign of any other footprint.

"We must have passed them in the gulch," decided

the Lone Ranger, "and yet I don't see how we could have."

Tonto was frankly puzzled. It had seemed, at first, that there could be no explanation for the fact that Rance Morgan was still alive, but this mystery had been cleared up. The hanging was simply a case of key men cooperating to stage an event that would mislead the witnesses. But the disappearance of Morgan and the lawyer was something that defied explanation. Men didn't dissolve in thin air!

While the Lone Ranger and Tonto stood there undecided as to whether or not they should retrace their steps and make a more thorough search, there came a sound that electrified them. It was the shrill cry of a horse. A peculiarly powerful cry that was long-drawn-out, almost like the anguished wail of a human. The cry was a familiar one that brought an exclamation from the masked man's lips.

"Silver!"

It was unmistakably the white stallion that whinnied. The sound echoed and re-echoed from the walls of the canyon. Heedless of danger to himself, oblivious to the fact that eyes of men and guns of death might at that very moment be trained on him, the Lone Ranger swung into the dense foliage and beat his way into the depths.

He beat a zigzag course between the cliffs, flailing with his arms, tearing away the plants and weeds that grew in his path.

"Silver!" the Lone Ranger cried. "Silver! Where are you, old fellow?"

The echo of his voice came back to mock him.

Tonto followed close behind the masked man.

Briars tore at the Lone Ranger's clothes and thorns raked his skin. He stumbled and almost fell over exposed roots, and several times sank halfway to his knees in sticky muck. The horse's cry was not repeated.

His breath came in burning gasps, and pains lanced his chest; he could feel his heart pounding with the strain of his efforts. But, heedlessly, the Lone Ranger continued his desperate investigation of Croyden's Gulch.

It took more than an hour for him to reach the furthermost end. Still unsatisfied, the masked man retraced his route while Tonto used the skill of his race trying to read some sign of a presence among the luxuriant ferns and underbrush.

Finally, exhausted and caked with mud and sweat and blood from innumerable scratches, the Lone Ranger and Tonto emerged from the gulch. The sun was almost directly overhead.

On the open plain the two tired men turned back to look again at the place of mystery. This obviously was defeat. Grimly the Lone Ranger accepted that there was nothing for them to do but to leave. On foot and unarmed the situation looked hopeless. Yet, the Lone Ranger would not accept defeat.

What supplies had not been packed on the horses were still cached in the woods a quarter of a mile away. Feeling like a deserter as he turned his back on the place where Silver had last been heard, the masked man led the way across the plains on foot.

CHAPTER XIII

ABERCROMBIE'S BOILED SHIRT

The success of Rance Morgan in his criminal career wasn't founded on anything so fickle as good luck or chance. It was founded on a rare understanding of other men; a brain that could foresee every possibility of failure and plan a way to circumvent it, and on an utterly conscienceless soul.

Just as he had known when first he called on Luther Abercrombie, that the lawyer could be brought to do anything—including murder, so he had realized long before that the surest way to preserve the goods he stole was to have a hiding place that could never be found.

Many criminals had met their downfall through the accident of someone blundering onto their sanctuary. Rance Morgan knew there would be no chance of his cave in Croyden's Gulch being discovered; no one used the gulch.

Even to gain access to the place himself, had necessitated a rope ladder that could be let down from the plateau. Thus he could go and come as he pleased, and still leave the entrance to his headquarters overgrown. He trusted no one. Only a few of his own men knew about the cave, and the loot that was there.

Another reason for Morgan's success was that he kept his men loyal by one means or another. Bat Kester had expected to be killed for squealing. Now he was dead. An occasional example of this sort had a decided effect on the other men with whom the leader dealt.

When he raced out of the gulch with Luther Abercrombie, Morgan didn't know that he was being followed. He forced the lawyer to climb up the swinging ladder, and when he, too, had reached the plateau, Morgan pulled the ladder up. It was thus that he disappeared, to the confusion of the Lone Ranger and Tonto.

The captured horses, Silver and Scout, had been taken by a devious trail to the plateau the night before. They had been left tied to stakes driven in the ground.

Morgan had kept Abercrombie with him to discuss plans for the future. He was delighted in his discovery of Luther Abercrombie. For a moment, after the trial, he had felt that his legal counsel left a lot to be desired, but that was before the conference in prison.

"It's just as I told you when I called on you the night before the hanging," Abercrombie said. "You've been legally hanged and pronounced dead. Now you are far removed from anything the law can do."

"It's swell," said Rance Morgan, "all but for one thing!"

"And what is that one thing?"

"The Lone Ranger. I've heard plenty about that man, an' the way he got loose from the cave makes me surer than ever that there's somethin' almost uncanny about the things he can do."

"Rot," sniffed the lawyer. "He's escaped, but what of that?"

"He knows that I'm alive. He's sure tuh know it."

"Granting that he knows it, what can he do about it?"

Rance Morgan shook his head. "I dunno."

"You follow my instructions," said Abercrombie, "and we'll have the whole town eating out of our hands."

"I did what you said last night, but I'd have felt a heap better about it if you hadn't made it a point that I let the sheriff get a look at me."

"Perhaps you don't realize how superstitious men are in this part of the country. I grant you, Morgan, you've done very well without me, but working together we can take over the entire town, perhaps the county. Who knows, we might control the state before we are finished."

"We been all over that before," said Morgan. "I'm convinced that you've got a pretty darn good head on your shoulders."

Abercrombie's lips pinched a smile. The two were on the level land above the gulch awaiting the arrival of men who were coming from Kerr's Corners.

"Just wait," said Abercrombie. "Wait until I go back and tell how all the men who came here disappeared in Croyden's Gulch; Jack Tilson and the others. No one has the slightest suspicion that they are taking orders from you. I promise you, Morgan, this will be called the Haunted Gulch when I finish my story. The Haunted Gulch over which a walking dead man watches."

"Meanin' me."

"Meaning you. Why all we will have to do is make a demand in your name! When the demand is refused, you'll strike in ways that baffle understanding. What you did before will be nothing compared to what we will do in the future."

"I still wish the Lone Ranger wasn't around here somewhere. When I seen that he'd got loose, I figured the best thing was to get away from that cave in a hurry. Now what are we goin' tuh do about him?"

"That is going to be simple."

"Well?"

"We are going to let the sheriff himself hunt down the Lone Ranger. You leave that to me."

"I've got to leave a lot of things to you." Rance Morgan wasn't entirely happy with the state of things.

The sound of horses brought Rance Morgan to his feet. "Here," he said, "come the boys."

"That's the signal for me to start back for town," responded Luther Abercrombie."

The four men on horses and one on the wagon drove up a rock-strewn trail that showed no tracks. As soon as they had been given their instructions they would circle to the plain below and leave a trail into the gulch. Their trail, backed up by what Luther Abercrombie planned to tell, would complete an impressive story.

Abercrombie was a sorry sight when he arrived in town at sunset. Going directly to the office of the sheriff, he dismounted slowly and painfully from the back of Jack Tilson's horse. He limped as he crossed the porch and walked through the office, to sink exhausted onto a chair near Jim Peabody.

"Wal!" exclaimed the sheriff. "This is a surprise. I reckon you got a lot tuh tell, but you just sit right there an' get yer breath. You look plumb tuckered out."

"I am. I've had the most harrowing experience you can imagine."

"Lone Ranger?"

"I wonder if it was the Lone Ranger who abducted me."

"I been wonderin' the same thing. Now unless you was an out an' out crook, the Lone Ranger wouldn't handle you like I was told he did."

"You heard about the way he forced an entry into my office and carried me away?"

"Sure thing. The boys went out huntin' you an' said the tracks just disappeared somewheres near the gulch."

"I don't know about the tracks of the Lone Ranger, I was unconscious. But there *is* something mightily weird—I might say supernatural about that gulch."

Abercrombie dropped his voice to a confidential tone

and leaned toward the big lawman. "Look at me, Peabody. Look right into my eyes. Tell me if I look like a man who is out of his mind."

Peabody shook his head.

"I'd be willing to believe a man who said that I was crazy. I can't believe the things I've seen. I can't believe them! I saw men, and horses, and a big wagon disappear into thin air."

Jim Peabody looked at the other dubiously. "Say that again."

"I saw five men, seven horses, and a wagon disappear."

"Where."

"At Croyden's Gulch."

"When?"

"About noon today."

"You sure you know what you're talkin' about, Abercrombie?"

"I am. Now let me tell you the most incredible thing you ever heard."

"Go ahead."

"After the Lone Ranger, if it was really he, took me away from town, he headed for Croyden's Gulch and plunged in among the weeds, the Indian behind him."

"Hold on, are yuh dead sure he went in?"

"Yes. He went in."

"Now hold on, Abercrombie. Jack Tilson followed

the trail as far as the gulch an' said the hoofmarks stopped, an' that there wasn't no sign of anyone havin' passed beyond the mouth."

"That's just one of the incredible things, Sheriff. I don't attempt to explain them, except to say that sometimes there are manifestations which are beyond the scope of ordinary mortals; spiritual and psychic phenomena that man cannot explain."

Peabody squirmed uneasily. "Get back tuh where you was."

"Now let me see." Abercrombie passed his hand across his forehead. He was really exhausted and acted even more so. "Where was I?"

"The Lone Ranger had taken you tuh the gulch."

"Oh, yes. Well, I heard Tilson and the others looking around. I wanted to cry out to them to come and save me, but I was gagged and helpless. I knew that were I to struggle that the savage Indian would strangle me—just as the masked man planned to strangle your prisoner."

"*What?*" Peabody fairly bellowed. "You say the masked man planned tuh strangle Bat Kester?"

"That was the talk. He said that he would remove his mask and get square with Kester."

"Jumpin' juniper, Mister Abercrombie. It was Rance Morgan that got Kester. You mean tuh say that the masked man an' Rance Morgan are . . ."

"I'm simply trying to give you the facts as I saw

them," Abercrombie said coldly. "I'm almost at the end of my rope, and I'll appreciate it if you don't interrupt me again."

"Go on, go on then. Tell me some more."

"The men rode away last night, Tilson and the others, without finding me there. Then, a little later, leaving me gagged and tied, the man you've been calling the Lone Ranger left me. I wormed my way along the ground, struggling all night long to escape. The ropes worked loose and I was able to remove the gag. At daybreak, I reached the mouth of the gulch and must have lost consciousness. I wakened with the sun high overhead. Jack Tilson was beside me."

"Him an' a posse set out at daybreak. They was goin' tuh clean out that gulch if need be an' try tuh locate you."

"I know. I told him about the masked man. Tilson told me about the death of Bat Kester. Then he and the others entered the gulch, cutting through some of the weeds to get the wagon in. I could hear them for a time. I had been told to wait or to borrow Tilson's horse and come back here. I hadn't long to wait when I heard the most awful screams coming from the men. I leaped to my feet and rushed toward them."

"What'd yuh see?"

"Nothing."

"*What?*"

"There was no sign of any of the men or the horses. Even the wagon was gone." Abercrombie snapped his fingers. "Just like that! The twinkling of an eye!"

The sheriff leaned back in his chair and mopped his sweaty forehead. "I—I cain't make it out," he said. "Rance Morgan, you say, is still alive?"

"I've given you the facts as I saw them." The lawyer made his voice impressive. "I have heard of things like this before, Peabody. I wouldn't say this to everyone for fear of being ridiculed, but you are a man of intelligence. You know that there are forces of nature that baffle man's knowledge and understanding."

Peabody nodded mechanically.

"It is my belief that Croyden's Gulch is . . . *haunted.*"

For a long time Jim Peabody sat in silence, deep in thought.

The story the lawyer had told was not in any way the truth. As a matter of fact, Jack Tilson and the others had helped concoct the story after the Lone Ranger and Tonto had been knocked out. Tilson had gone back to town with every intention of taking some of the men Rance Morgan needed most to form his posse in the morning. Now those men were with Morgan, ready to aid in the further plottings of the gang. The sheriff would give an awe-inspiring story of their disappearance.

The Lone Ranger would be looked upon as a criminal, as Rance Morgan somehow returned from the dead. He would be shot on sight. It was a well-planned story Luther Abercrombie told, but he had made one mistake. Not even the sheriff noticed the discrepancy.

A man in nondescript attire had heard it, though. He was on the sheriff's porch, idling away the time by whittling at a stick. His keen hearing easily caught the things that were said. The stranger had been at the Morgan trial. After that he had disappeared. This evening he'd been in town for just a few moments before the arrival of Luther Abercrombie.

He rose to his feet and opened the door.

Jim Peabody turned, then said, "I'm busy, go 'way."

"I just wanted to borrow a pencil and paper for a minute, Sheriff."

"Now you get—"

"Won't take a minute," insisted the stranger as he took the articles he wanted off the desk. He scribbled a hasty note, then handed it to the lawman.

"What's this?"

"Read it."

The sheriff glanced at the note. A look of surprise came over his face. Then he pursed his lips in thought and frowned while Abercrombie rose to his feet.

"I'll go home now, I need sleep."

"Just one minute, Abercrombie. There's just one thing more I want to ask you."

"Well, please be brief."

"You said you'd spent the night crawlin' along the ground in the gulch."

"Yes. What of it?"

"You got a habit of wearin' boiled shirts like that one you got on right now."

"Of course. I trust no one objects," returned the lawyer with an acid tongue.

Peabody shook his head slowly. "I ain't objectin' tuh the way you dress, but that shirt sure as thunder ain't in the right condition this minute."

"Why not?"

The sheriff pinched the cracked and mud-marked shirt between his big thumb and forefinger. "Starch," he said. "Still starchy in spite of all the wearin' it's had. Now there's a loose screw somewhere in yer story because it rained cats an' dogs last night an' if you was out in it that there shirt would be some different!"

Luther Abercrombie became a panther. His lips snapped back from yellow teeth that almost looked like fangs. With speed that was almost incredible he snatched a gun from beneath his coat, and fired.

The stranger in the dusty clothes leaped forward, but quick as he was, Abercrombie was quicker.

The lawyer had the advantage of surprise. He seemed to have sensed what was coming when the sheriff started the sequence of questions. He had fired, then thrown the gun toward the stranger and streaked through the open door screaming at the top of his voice.

"Murder! Murder! Come quick!"

The door slammed behind Luther Abercrombie, but the stranger could hear his shrill cries, and the responding shouts of men who seemed to be coming on the run from all directions.

"The sheriff has been murdered! Come here! Get the killer!"

Jim Peabody's heavy legs were wobbling. His eyes stared unbelievingly at the blood that seeped through his fingers as he clutched at his bulging stomach. Then he collapsed upon the floor.

CHAPTER XIV

THE SHERIFF MUST DIE

The Lone Ranger and Tonto had been at a complete disadvantage when they were in the gulch. One startling event had come so close on the heels of another that there had been no chance for them to gather their dazed senses. They had witnessed the appearance of Rance Morgan, but it had been hard to concentrate on what Morgan and Abercrombie said.

The realization of the extent of Rance Morgan's power in Kerr's Corners made the Lone Ranger aware of the possible hopelessness of proving the man alive, and of bringing all his satellites to justice.

After the disappearance of Rance Morgan and Luther Abercrombie, the Lone Ranger and Tonto had pushed their bruised bodies far beyond the point of fatigue in the frantic hunt for Silver.

It wasn't until the two had returned to their camp in the woods and refreshed themselves that they were able to apply their usual sound reasoning to the problems at hand. Tonto listened attentively while the Lone Ranger did the talking and planning.

"We know," the masked man had said, "that Silver is near here, even though he isn't in the gulch. I heard him and I'd know his cry anywhere. The chances are that Silver and Scout are together. You'll stay around here, perhaps at the edge of the woods, where you can keep an eye on the entrance to the gulch. If anyone tries to ride Silver, there'll be a terrific rumpus. You might get the chance to locate the horses."

There was a rifle in the camp that Tonto could use as a weapon. The Lone Ranger went on with his plans.

"While you're watching for the horses, I'm going to go back to town. We learned that Abercrombie is going there and I intend to keep close tabs on him. I'll wear the same old clothes I wore the last time, and use the old six-gun that goes with those clothes."

These plans had been carried out. The Lone Ranger had gone on foot to Kerr's Corners, arriving there about the same time that Luther Abercrombie tied the deputy sheriff's horse at the hitch rack and visited Jim Peabody.

A few moments later the Lone Ranger found himself in a critical situation. It was he who stood over the prostrate form of the sheriff while Luther Abercrombie screamed for help.

The disguised man had to think fast. He knew that his word, the word of a stranger, would carry no weight against the story the lawyer would tell. Unquestionably, he would be accused of shooting Jim Peabody, and nothing would convince the townsmen otherwise.

In fact, the closer the townsmen investigated him,

the more likely they were to find that some of the hair in his heavy eyebrows, and his mustache as well, was false. At best he would be legally hanged, but the odds were in favor of his being lynched at once.

Heavy steps clattered on the porch. The door started to swing in when the Lone Ranger threw his weight against it. He heard a bedlam of shouts from outside as he dropped a heavy bar in place.

"Open up," cried someone. "Open up or we'll shoot our way in."

The Lone Ranger ignored the cries. He crossed the room in two long strides then dropped beside the fallen sheriff. It took but a second to learn that the lawman was still alive. The wound was in the stomach. It might or might not prove fatal. The Lone Ranger had to know.

Someone outside fired a shot that tore a big chunk from the door.

"That's just a warnin'."

The Lone Ranger barely heard the yells and threats. His powerful fingers tore the sheriff's clothes aside to expose the flesh where the bullet had struck. "Not too bad," muttered the mysterious figure. "He should get well if there is no infection. Tonto could fix him."

Glass shattered into the room and a man's head and shoulders showed in the opening of the window.

The Lone Ranger threw himself to one side as a gun's roar filled the room. The bullet streaked too close.

The next shot would surely get him. He snatched up the gun from the floor where Abercrombie had tossed it and threw it straight at the man in the window.

There was a shout of pain as the heavy weapon caught the townsman on the side of the head. He dropped from view.

The assault on the door continued. The men outside were using something as a battering ram. The heavy timbers of the door creaked and bent beneath the pounding.

There was a chance, a slim chance of escape.

The Lone Ranger waited for another crash. It came. Then he silently lifted the bar from the sockets in which it rested and gently lifted the latch. The door was free to swing in easily under the lightest pressure. The next blow of the battering ram sent the portal flying back, and a dozen men who held the big rail of the hitch rack went sprawling across the floor of the office.

A lean, lithe figure leaped upon the fallen men, jumped over them and almost dove headfirst to the porch. Two men reached to grab him. He drove a hard fist at the stomach of the first, and lunged sideways to bump the second man off balance.

The men on the floor were snatching at their guns as the Lone Ranger jumped across the railing of the porch, dashed at the nearest horse, and vaulted over the animal's rump.

Half a dozen pistols spoke at once, but the shots were wild.

Even as he touched the saddle, the Lone Ranger brought his hand down on the flank of the borrowed horse and dug his heels into its sides.

Surprised and frightened, the horse leaped ahead, almost running wild. The Lone Ranger bent low over the neck of the chestnut mare. Townsmen, infuriated at the escape of the man they thought had killed the sheriff, streaked toward their own horses and took to the saddle in hot pursuit.

There had been no time for the Lone Ranger to select his horse, he had been forced to take the nearest one. Within the first two hundred yards of riding, he realized that the choice had been a bad one. The mare, after its first frightened burst of speed, leveled to a steady gait that was far too slow to keep ahead of pursuers for very long.

However his head start had put the Lone Ranger far enough in advance of those who pursued him to make the risk of being shot by pistol fire practically negligible—for the moment. The townsmen seemed to realize this, because they held their fire and devoted their energies to closing in on the fugitive.

It was only a matter of minutes.

The Lone Ranger shouted cries of encouragement to the mare. He slapped at the broad rump with his hat. The speed remained constant.

He didn't fire. He couldn't. His code placed a firm taboo on the taking of a human life, even the life of a murderer. And those who were coming on from behind were not murderers; they were townsmen, the very people for whom the mysterious figure of the West was fighting Rance Morgan and his schemes.

It would, perhaps, have been better to have halted, held up his hands, and surrendered. But quitting was a thing that never entered the Lone Ranger's mind.

He pressed on with frequent glances at the constantly shortening gap between him and the dozen men who pounded after him.

Looking ahead again, he saw something that brought a sudden throb to his throat. Coming toward him were two other horses. At first, he couldn't believe what he saw. It couldn't be—yet it was. No horse in all the West had the stride of the white stallion that raced toward him led by the Indian who rode on the paint.

"Tonto," breathed the Lone Ranger. "Tonto and Scout . . . and *Silver*."

Another glance behind showed the pursuing men nearer than he had realized. They were firing now, and at a range that was close enough to make those barking guns a genuine threat.

Tonto grasped the situation instantly. He brought the horses to a halt. He turned them, then tossed the reins, by which he had led the mighty Silver, over the horse's head and across the pommel of the saddle.

The Lone Ranger guided the chestnut alongside Silver. "Come on, Silver," he shouted.

Silver fell into the stride with the mare, running close beside her. The Lone Ranger rose from the saddle. He leaned out, grasped the pommel, threw himself across the gap and landed in his own familiar saddle. Wonder of wonders, his cartridge belts and guns swung from the pommel.

"We go now," Tonto cried.

The Lone Ranger was off with his familiar ringing cry, "Hi-Yo, Silver! Away!"

Silver became a flashing streak. White mane and tail flew like silken banners in the wind. Every stride made the chase more hopeless for the men behind.

Tonto grinned widely at his friend. This was one of those moments that made all hardships seem worth while: the Lone Ranger on his great horse Silver, putting distance between him and those who sought to kill him.

It was a mere matter of minutes before the men from Kerr's Corners realized the futility of further chase and turned to head back home with the chestnut mare.

Back in the town, Luther Abercrombie watched while the doctor examined Jim Peabody's wound.

"He'll get well," the doctor reported. "It's nothin' too serious."

"I'm afraid you're mistaken, Doctor," said the lawyer softly.

"Mistaken? No such thing. I'll have the sheriff on his feet an' well as ever in a couple of weeks."

Luther Abercrombie shook his head. "You can't."

"Why not?"

"You won't."

"But I—" the doctor broke off as he saw the expression in the lawyer's face.

"You said that Rance Morgan was dead. Remember?"

"Y-yes, but I had to. You told me what'd happen if I didn't."

"You've got some money coming to you, Doctor. You'll have more—after the poor sheriff dies."

"But if that stranger in town shot him like folks say—"

"That," said Abercrombie softly, "is why the sheriff must not regain consciousness. He is the only one who *knows* who shot him."

The doctor's eyes went wide. "Y-you mean to say—"

A nod. "The wound is fatal. Do you understand? *The sheriff must die!*"

There was a long pause. The eyes of the two professional men met in a challenge. The doctor was torn between his ethics as a doctor and love of his own life. He knew what would happen to him if he defied the mandate of the lawyer. Rance Morgan still lived. Death stalked any man who defied Morgan or any of his representatives.

The physician nodded slowly, despising himself for his weakness. "I—I guess," he faltered, "you're right. That wound is fatal. There's nothin' a doctor can do for a man that's hurt like poor Jim Peabody. The sheriff will die!"

Luther Abercrombie smiled and nodded.

CHAPTER XV

TONTO'S STORY

The Lone Ranger, racing across the plains, felt his spirits rise in a mighty upsurge from the lowest point of hopelessness to the peak of confidence.

Wind brushed his face and lashed his neckerchief until it crackled like a whip. His own heavy guns were strapped in place, and their weight felt good against his thighs. It was glorious to be aboard the dependable Silver once again and know that there was no horse in all the West that could overtake him. How his sharp hoofs beat the turf! How the long, powerful legs drove horse and rider forward! Best of all, Tonto rode beside him, and Tonto was grinning!

But there were problems, many of them, still ahead of the Lone Ranger. It seemed almost hopeless to expect to capture every member of the Rance Morgan gang. Circumstances had made it unsafe to go into town again. In his disguise, the Lone Ranger was hunted as the stranger who had shot Jim Peabody; as the Lone Ranger himself, the Morgan gang would certainly hunt him down now that he had escaped from the gulch.

But with Silver and his weapons, the mystery rider felt equal to anything.

Riding at top speed, he shouted a brief explanation of the flight from town. He told Tonto how the sheriff had been shot by Luther Abercrombie, and how Abercrombie had managed to shift the blame.

"One thing I'm sure of," he called to the man who rode beside him. "If the sheriff lives he'll tell the truth about the lawyer. He knows that Abercrombie's story of what happened in the gulch is not true. That's why we can't go far; we've got to circle back as soon as we're sure the men behind have given up the chase. If he can, Abercrombie will see to it that the sheriff doesn't live."

Tonto said something about the doctor, but the Lone Ranger reminded him that the doctor had already proved himself dishonest when he had pronounced Rance Morgan dead.

The two turned the horses toward the north and rode for almost a mile before making another right turn, and heading back in the general direction of Kerr's Corners.

Tonto explained his part of the afternoon's activities. He had remained in the camp for some time after the Lone Ranger had left for town. Finally he had gone to the edge of the woods and sat on the ground where he could watch the distant gulch. On his left there was the hill and the false grave of Rance Morgan; straight ahead, across level land, he saw the entrance to the gulch, and, on each side of this, steep sloping hills that rose to table land.

Tonto studied the plateau. It was too high for him to see beyond the edge, but he wondered what might be there and considered the idea of investigating. The more he studied the geologic structure, the more he felt convinced that the cry of a horse on the plateau might easily sound as though it came from the gulch itself.

He was about to move toward the place when he saw two men come from the direction of the town leading a horse. The horse, a nondescript chestnut of moderate size, was not one of the two for which the Indian was on watch. The men, however, were of great interest to Tonto. They were Luther Abercrombie and Rance Morgan.

The plotters walked slowly and appeared to be in earnest conversation. Some distance from the entrance to the gulch they halted, and the lawyer mounted the horse. After several moments of further conversation, Luther Abercrombie turned the horse, and started back in the direction from which he had come. His route was one that would take him to Kerr's Corners.

Before the horseman had gone far, Rance Morgan headed for the steep wall at one side of the entrance to the gulch and started climbing.

From Tonto's point of view no trail was visible, but there must have been one because Morgan seemed to have no difficulty. He ascended rapidly to the rim of the plateau, only to disappear.

Tonto ran forward carrying his rifle. He reached the

place where he'd seen the two men talking and found their footprints clearly defined in the ground that had been softened by the recent rains.

He saw and studied the marks which Rance Morgan had made and followed these to the place where the outlaw had scaled the wall. There the Indian stood perplexed. There wasn't the slightest foothold on the slippery clay that faced the plain! Tonto looked up at the ledge far above his head. How could any human being climb up there? It seemed impossible, yet Rance Morgan had done it!

Tonto felt challenged. He tried to find a place to grip the wall with his strong fingers. There was no such place. He couldn't climb two feet off the ground! Yet Morgan had climbed a hundred feet and reached the top.

Frustrated, Tonto turned back to study the tracks once more. He determined to follow them back and reach the point from which Morgan and Abercrombie had come.

The tracks were easily followed. Tonto, had he had a horse, could have ridden at top speed and still discerned the marks of men and a horse. For a time the hoofmarks of the chestnut horse going toward Kerr's Corners were close to those which had been made in reaching the place at the base of the cliff. Then there was a branch. The back trail that Tonto was following now branched off to the left.

That was when Tonto made his discovery. He hadn't

noticed it before, but the cliff had been constantly diminishing in height until it merged into the plain. The back trail led in a complete half circle. Tonto found himself walking back toward the gulch, but this time he was near the edge of the plateau. Suddenly he saw a sight that brought a quick emotional jerk to his throat. Ahead, ten minutes walk ahead, there were two large horses. One was Scout and the other was unquestionably Silver!

Exerting extreme caution, Tonto scouted further. Beyond the horses there were men, six of them, and one was Rance Morgan. Also there were other horses, and a large, heavy wagon. The Indian crept forward another fifty yards and dropped flat on his belly. If Scout or Silver happened to see him they would register the fact and those well-armed men with Morgan would come gunning.

Several times Tonto saw Silver's ears cocked forward; the big horse seemed to sense the presence of a friend. At these times the Indian hugged the ground and remained motionless until he saw the heavy stallion relax. Then he squirmed a trifle nearer.

Morgan and the others appeared to be busy at a strange task. They were gathered around the big wagon, backing it toward the edge of the gulch. Tonto could hear a shout of *"Now."* The men gave a mighty shove then stepped back quickly while the rig rolled over the edge and crashed down among the trees.

Tonto snaked closer. He could hear the voices now,

and was close enough to recognize a couple of the men as deputies appointed by the sheriff. One, in fact, was the deputy whose gun he had shot away in front of Luther Abercrombie's office.

"Abercrombie will spread the story around town," Rance Morgan was saying, "he'll pay off some of the men that helped us, an' tell how you boys an' the horses disappeared. That'll keep folks away from the gulch from now on."

"What about the Lone Ranger an' that Injun that escaped with him?"

"I got that all fixed, too," answered Morgan. "The only trouble is that I can't get aboard the Lone Ranger's horse, but that won't matter much. I'll find another white horse that'll do."

The deputy named Tilson was looking at the overcast sky. "We'll come out all right on the rain," he said. "There'll be more rain for sure before mornin'."

"Good enough. That'll wash out the tracks."

Tonto ventured a little closer to the group. Once more Silver's ears jerked to attention. This time Scout, too, seemed to sense the nearness of the Indian. Nostrils of both horses quivered slightly and their heads cocked sideways.

Tonto was far from satisfied. He still didn't know how Rance Morgan had scaled the slippery wall or how Morgan and Abercrombie had disappeared so completely from the gulch.

These questions were answered by Rance Morgan

who reached for what appeared to be a tangled mass of heavy rope that lay near the edge of the plateau.

"I'll drop the rope ladder down near the cave," he said. "You boys climb down an' settle yourselves in the cave, then I'll pull the ladder up an' when the next rain washes out these other tracks you'll all have disappeared so's there'll be a real mystery about this place." He added, "I'll take care of the horses."

Then things happened. Silver at last found his suspicions justified. He caught a glimpse of Tonto and whinnied loudly, rearing on his hind legs as he did so.

The men wheeled at the sound and looked about them. It was time for Tonto to act without delay. If Morgan and his men had time to bring their guns to bear or mount their horses, they'd dispose of the Indian in short order.

Tonto leaped to his feet and shouted, "Here, Silver. Come quick, Scout."

Surprised shouts broke from the men. Several snatched at guns and fired without taking time to aim. Jack Tilson was more methodical, he steadied his gun and drew a careful bead on Tonto.

Meanwhile Silver and Scout reared and plunged, throwing their weight against the straining ropes that held them to stakes in the ground.

Tonto brought his rifle up and fired. His aim didn't suffer by its suddenness. Tilson's pistol flew from his hand like a thing that had suddenly been imbued with life. The deputy cursed loudly.

Silver and Scout raced side by side to Tonto. They didn't have to break their stride when they reached the Indian. Tonto leaped at Scout as the paint horse approached, and threw one shot behind him as he raced away.

"Gittum up, Scout," shouted the Indian, knowing that Silver would maintain any pace that Scout could set.

Tonto made a discovery that pleased him immensely as he raced away from the bullets that buzzed around him. Dangling from the pommel of the saddles, he saw the guns that had been taken from him and the Lone Ranger. He let Scout have his head, while he used both hands to strap his own gun belt around his waist. Then he made sure that the Lone Ranger's guns were well secured and dashed toward Kerr's Corners.

Tonto had no special plan in mind. He only knew that the Lone Ranger was probably still in town and judged that the horses would be welcome.

He didn't know until he met his disguised friend riding toward him, a leap ahead of the pursuing citizens, how badly the great speed of Silver was needed.

It took some time for Tonto to finish his story. He had to shout it, to be heard above the thundering hoofs of the horses. By the time he had finished the town was once again in sight and darkness had fallen.

"I hope," cried the Lone Ranger, "we're not too late to save the sheriff's life."

"That Tonto hope," replied the other, referring to himself in the third person as he frequently did.

Tonto's recital answered many questions that had lodged in the Lone Ranger's mind. The many complications of Rance Morgan's extensive plans and schemes were fitting themselves into one vast pattern for crime on a county-wide, and perhaps a state-wide, scale.

The two riders halted behind a row of buildings and dismounted. Tonto held back while the Lone Ranger stepped into the shadows and, crouching, moved toward a lighted window.

CHAPTER XVI

THE NEW LONE RANGER

It was the sheriff's office that the Lone Ranger and Tonto approached in the darkness. Through the window the two could see a group of men who seemed to be discussing the recent shooting of the lawman.

The voices reached the Lone Ranger clearly. He saw nothing of the sheriff, but all the talk dealt with the oversized lawman.

"I hope," thought the Lone Ranger, "we aren't too late. If Abercrombie and the doctor have had their way, Peabody will have breathed his last by this time."

Someone in the room was saying, "I never seen a woman like her."

"Well, we done what she wanted, but as fer me I hope I don't have tuh tote him in his casket. By juniper, he shore weighs aplenty."

"I dunno what come over Jim's wife. She run in here like a tornado an' looked at Big Jim. She seen that he was still breathin'. Then she started givin' orders like all git out."

The men appeared to be explaining things to others who had just joined the group in the office.

"Is he dead or alive?" wondered the Lone Ranger.

One of the men inside continued. "She wouldn't

listen tuh the Doc or Abercrombie or anyone else. She jest said, 'Move 'im.' So we done it."

"We done it all right an' because o' that my arms will sure be achin' fer the next week."

"Why'd Ma Peabody want him toted home, anyhow?"

"I dunno. The doctor told her that he'd have tuh do some operatin' on the sheriff an' she says that he could do it at the house as well as here. Doc argued with her, but he didn't git nowheres at all. I reckon he's doin' his work on Jim right now."

"How about the man that shot the sheriff?"

The Lone Ranger heard no more. He motioned to Tonto, and the two dodged quickly and unnoticed around one side of the office, and across the road. They moved to the rear of the sheriff's home and advanced to a lighted window.

"I think this is where Jim sleeps," whispered the Lone Ranger.

"That right," said Tonto. The Indian knew much about Jim Peabody's public and private life. In fact, Tonto had made it his business to learn all he could about everyone in Kerr's Corners.

The Lone Ranger crouched beneath the window then removed his hat and raised himself until his eyes could peer over the sill.

The room beyond the glass was lighted by an oil lamp that rested on a small washstand. Jim's huge bulk filled a bed and mounded the blankets. His wife stood next to him with a look of defiance in her face.

"Anything you need tuh do with Jim, you go right ahead an' do while I'm watchin' you," the woman said to the doctor.

"But, Mrs. Peabody," protested the man of medicine, "I—I've got tuh—well tuh sort of operate on him. I—I'm not used tuh workin' with folks around. I—I might uh . . . er—I might git nervous."

"You do what's gotta be done."

"Besides that," continued the doctor with an agitated voice, "it mightn't be good fer a woman tuh watch." He shifted his weight uneasily and fumbled with the instruments in his bag which rested on a chair.

"I can stand watchin' anything that's done to Jim." Ma Peabody's stand was a determined one. Her arms were crossed and she kept steady eyes on the nervous movements of the doctor.

"I've seen you workin' before now," the woman continued, "an' I ain't any too much confidence in you. Now go ahead an' patch my husband up, an' see that you do a first-class job of it."

The doctor crossed the room and lifted one arm of the unconscious man. As he held the wrist, counting the pulse, the door of the room opened and Luther Abercrombie showed himself.

"How is he now?" inquired the lawyer.

The doctor shook his head slowly. Ma Peabody

didn't notice anything significant in the look that was exchanged between the doctor and the lawyer, but the Lone Ranger saw it through the window and understood.

The Lone Ranger himself knew that the sheriff's wound was not nearly as serious as it might have been. Without help, the sheriff would recover unless his resistance was much lower than his ruddy appearance indicated or unless infection set in. With Tonto's help, the lawman would be practically certain of full and complete recovery. Yet, there stood the doctor with his bag of gleaming instruments and orders to make sure the man on the bed never regained consciousness.

Luther Abercrombie seemed to catch the meaning in the doctor's glance. To the woman he said, "I'd like to speak to you for a moment, Mrs. Peabody, would you mind stepping into the other room?"

It was on the Lone Ranger's lips to shout out, "Don't go," but he dared not betray his presence. He could have cheered when he heard the sheriff's wife say, "You're darned tootin' I'd mind."

"But, Madam—"

"Don't 'but' me. There ain't a thing you can say that's more important tuh me than stayin' right here alongside Jim. Now tell that sawbones tuh git tuh work an' bring my husband around tuh consciousness so he can tell me all about what happened in his office."

"I," said the lawyer, "can tell you just what happened. I was there and a witness to everything."

"I don't believe anything I hear from anyone but Jim. Now fix him up an' be quick about it." Ma Peabody addressed the latter part of her speech to the doctor.

Arguments continued in the room. The Lone Ranger turned to Tonto and whispered quick instructions. Tonto at first looked surprised, but quickly understood the reason for the request, and slipped away from the window.

The Lone Ranger glanced inside once more and saw the sheriff showing signs of returning consciousness. Luther Abercrombie tried hard to control the tense expression of his face.

The sheriff's lips moved slightly as he tried to speak. His wife hurried close to him and bent over. She straightened and poured water from a pitcher to a glass and held this to Jim's lips.

The doctor stepped forward at that point and almost shoved the woman to the side. "Let me see him," he said hurriedly. "This might be the end. He looks as if he's slippin' fast."

"But there's things he's tryin' to tell me!"

"Not now, not now," snapped the doctor. "I must work fast if I'm to save him. We've spent too much time in argument already." With fire that was unusual in the doctor, he barked at Luther Abercrombie. "Get that woman out of here. I can't let this man die."

"I certainly will!"

Abercrombie grabbed Ma Peabody and fairly threw

her through the door with a strength that was surprising in so lean a man. It must have been the strength born of desperation. If the sheriff talked it would be the lawyer who would be accused of shooting with intent to kill. This must not happen.

The doctor pulled the door closed on the struggling couple and turned a key in the lock.

Jim was trying hard to sit up in the bed. The doctor's hands fairly flew as he dipped into his bag and brought up a bottle of brightly colored pills.

"Now take it easy, Jim," he said. "I'm right here alongside you an' we're going to pull you through."

"Where is my wife?" demanded the sheriff.

"She'll be right in. Just take this pill."

Ma Peabody could be heard beyond the door. She was shouting her rage and fury against a softer background of the lawyer's voice which he tried to make sound consoling.

"Bring Ma in here," said the sheriff.

"Right away, Jim, just as soon as you take this pill. Here's water to go with it."

The Lone Ranger felt that he could wait no longer for Tonto to come back with the article he needed. The pill the doctor held to big Jim's lips was probably a poison. Jim opened his mouth—the Lone Ranger acted.

The glass panes in the window splintered in a thousand tiny pieces on the floor of the bedroom as the Lone Ranger leaped through the opening. As he leaped he swept the doctor to one side.

Surprised, the doctor stumbled backward and would have fallen to the floor, if he hadn't been blocked by the corner of the room.

"That pill," cried the Lone Ranger, "is poison."

Jim was wide-eyed with surprise.

"They've told it around town that I'm the one who shot you, Sheriff. You know better than that. That's why you've got to get out of here with me. You're in serious danger."

The sheriff's lips were moving, but no sound came from them.

Abercrombie hammered on the door which had been locked by the doctor. His voice shrilled loud demands for admission to the room.

"I've got to make you understand, Sheriff," barked the Lone Ranger. "You're going to be killed. You've got to get away from here."

The doctor leaped forward with a shining scalpel in his hand and a wild look in his eyes. "I'll fix you," he cried.

The Lone Ranger stepped back, ducked, then lunged forward. He brought his fist around in a short jab that fairly whistled beneath the doctor's outstretched hand and whammed with stunning force against his unguarded chin.

The doctor's head snapped back. Once more he slammed into the corner of the room. This time his legs failed him and he slumped to a heap on the floor.

From outside there came a clatter of hoofs and a

rattle of wheels. Tontó had returned from his errand and the Lone Ranger breathed a sigh of relief. He ignored the cries that came from Ma Peabody and the lawyer on the other side of the locked door. He ignored the feeble resistance of Jim Peabody.

Tonto climbed through the shattered window and helped the tall man haul the heavy sheriff from the bed.

"Give us what help you can," the Lone Ranger told the lawman. "We have a wagon outside. We're getting you out of town where you'll have a fighting chance to live."

There was such conviction in the resonant tone of the Lone Ranger that the sheriff obeyed blindly. He staggered to the window and just managed to squirm through it. Tonto had gone through ahead of him and helped from the outside.

Abercrombie was trying to smash in the door of the room. Once, twice, and three times, he threw his meager weight against it without accomplishing his purpose. By the time he bumped the door once more, the Lone Ranger and Tonto were in the wagon with the barely conscious sheriff, ready to dash to a safety that was no more than comparative.

The Lone Ranger was about to call to the horses, when he froze in his seat. He heard a voice, a voice that came from somewhere in the front of the house. "Hi-Yo, Silver," was the cry he heard. His *own* cry. What did it mean?

Close on the heels of the call there came a burst of gunfire. More shots crashed in the night accompanied by shouts of men and fast hoofbeats.

"Stop him, stop him! That's the same one that was here before. Kill him!"

The Lone Ranger and Tonto waited rigidly in the wagon to which their horses had been hitched. The hard-riding fugitive, whoever he was, was coming nearer.

"I know the white horse," someone shouted. Another voice broke out yelling, "it's the Lone Ranger."

The real Lone Ranger tensed at the cry. Whoever the rider was, whatever he had done, the townsmen were convinced it was the Lone Ranger who had fired his guns, then raced away.

The hoofbeats receded with half a dozen men on horseback in pursuit. Their shouts of anger proved that they would shoot to kill for whatever the impostor had done.

The real Lone Ranger's voice was low when he said "Come on, Scout." He slapped the reins across the horses' rumps. "Come on, Silver."

The wagon carrying the sheriff who had lapsed again into unconsciousness moved slowly away.

Kerr's Corners was truly a dangerous place for the Lone Ranger now. In his mask, or in his nondescript disguise, he'd be shot on sight.

CHAPTER XVII

PREPARE TO DIE

Under cover of the shooting and shouting it was a simple matter for the Lone Ranger and Tonto to steal out of town with the wagon and the sheriff. By the time Luther Abercrombie found that the lawman had been taken out the window, the wagon was lost in darkness and excited cries about the fake Lone Ranger filled the street.

Abercrombie left the doctor lying in a limp heap in a corner of the bedroom. Cursing vividly, the lawyer dashed out of the house and away from the sheriff's sobbing wife.

The Lone Ranger, meanwhile, turned the reins over to Tonto. "Take the horses and the wagon to the place we picked out," he said hurriedly. "I'll join you there later on."

"Where you go?"

"I'm going back where we came from. I want to know more about this man who masqueraded as the Lone Ranger."

"It not safe. Feller in town shoot you because you capture sheriff."

"That's a chance I'll have to take, Tonto. I'll strip off the mustache, batter this old hat into a different shape,

136

and keep out of the light as much as possible. You take care of the sheriff and remember that he's the only man alive who knows that Abercrombie is a crook."

Tonto said, "Me fix-um wound."

The Lone Ranger knew that the simple statement of his Indian friend meant more than any pledge or wordy contract. He leaped lightly from the wagon and ran at a dogtrot back to town.

Every building was brightly lighted and yellow beams shone out to light the street. Everyone in town was out and almost everyone was talking. The air literally buzzed with excited conversation.

The Lone Ranger spotted the doctor, and noted with a certain inward satisfaction that the man looked very much disheveled. He followed him as far as the general store where a mass of people gaped in morbid curiosity at an old man's body lying face up on the floor.

"Let me in there," snarled the doctor. "I've got to see the remains."

The crowd gave way and the doctor strode through. The Lone Ranger listened closely to what was said and piece by piece he learned the story of old Hank Caulkins's death.

A man had ridden up on a white horse. The man's face was covered by a mask. He had drawn two guns on entering, and held them on the white-haired proprietor.

"Cash," he had demanded. "All you've got here, and make it fast."

Hank Caulkins had had no cash and said so. The

masked man hadn't been convinced and shouted for Liz Caulkins to come from the living quarters in back of the store.

Liz came through the glass-bead curtains and, like her husband, had denied the existence of any hoarded wealth.

"Don't try to put me off," the masked man had stormed. "You've heard of the Lone Ranger. I'm not a man to be fooled. Now hand out the cash or take the consequences."

A moment later there was a shot and the masked man raced away while poor old Hank gasped his last.

The real Lone Ranger seethed inwardly at the brutality of the impostor. He felt that now he would almost be justified in taking human life. Human? No, the man who had shot Hank Caulkins could not, by any stretch of the imagination, be called a human being. He was a monster, a craven being with a distorted mind and a heart like that of a vampire, craving life's blood.

There were many in the crowd who were dubious about the story. "It don't sound right," said one man within the hearing of the Lone Ranger. "I've been told aplenty about that there Lone Ranger an' none of it was anything like what's been done here."

"Me, too," said a grizzled old-timer with a battered blue hat of the union army. "Why, thunderation, the Lone Ranger never took a life. An' he don't go 'bout robbin' folks like this."

"Jest the same, the man that done this wore a mask an' rid a white hoss an' called himself the Lone Ranger, an' that's enough fer me. When I see him, if I'm lucky enough tuh do that same, I'm shootin' him as quick or quicker'n I would a pizen rattler that's about tuh bite my wife."

"Mebbe 'taint the Lone Ranger that done this. Mebbe 'taint the Lone Ranger that's here in town."

A nasal, twanging voice broke in shrilly. "Oh yes it is."

"Mister Abercrombie."

"You can depend on what I tell you. I guess everyone around here knows that I was carried away by that masked man." He looked at the settlers. "You knew about that?"

A couple of nods. "We knowed, sure we knowed."

"Then ask *me* if it's an impostor or the real Lone Ranger. I'll give you the answer. It is no impostor. It's the Lone Ranger with the horse named Silver—with the silver bullets—with the mask!"

Men shook their heads slowly. "By gum, I jest can't believe it."

"I'll tell you how you can believe it," went on the lawyer. "There are a number of things I must tell. You come with me and I'll tell you things that will make you shudder and tremble in real fear!"

"Gosh sakes," said one of the men in awe.

Luther Abercrombie had a magnificent command of words and a stately manner when he needed it to put on an impressive show. He had planned his evening with care. Men of influence in town were told that the lawyer had an amazing story that everyone should hear; they were invited to his office to listen, to hold council and make plans for the future.

The lawyer's office was jammed with men. Luther Abercrombie himself was not there. He bathed and changed to fresh clothing, and purposely kept his audience waiting to build up the element of suspense.

In a small room off the lawyer's office, the doctor listened to instructions, nodded, and went in to face the assembled townsmen.

The doctor gave a short introductory talk, explaining that the lawyer had been through a frightful experience, and that his health demanded rest and medical care. Abercrombie, however, motivated by his keen interest in the welfare of the town, had insisted, so the doctor declared, on relating certain facts which must be known before he would agree to take the richly deserved rest.

The townsmen's faces were serious. Any levity there might have been because of the excitement of the night was wiped away by the doctor's grim manner.

At that dramatic moment, the door at the side of the room swung open, and Luther Abercrombie stalked in slowly and sank into his chair.

The big clock in the corner ticked slowly with the heavy pendulum's ponderous swing. It was the only sound in the hushed room as the lawyer studied the men in front of him. He noted with satisfaction that the group included almost every man of any importance in the town.

Two windows on one side of the room which stood open were packed with the faces of men outside who hadn't been able to crowd into the office.

Bong! The sudden chiming of the clock startled the assemblage. A dozen heads turned and noticed that it was exactly midnight. Eleven more times the big clock sounded forth.

"Accidental," thought the lawyer with satisfaction, "but it is good that this meeting is being held at the stroke of midnight. It makes it much more impressive." He cleared his throat with the last of the chimes, then spoke with studied slowness and a choice of words that was almost too meticulous.

"Gentlemen, you may have heard about Rance Morgan's return from the dead to kill Bat Kester. We are all led to believe that death is a permanent thing. Morgan has proved that this is not the case. Now, while I don't wish to alarm you needlessly, circumstances have developed which make it a necessity for us of Kerr's Corners to take precautions.

"History is filled with stories of events which cannot be explained. We are living near a gulch that is generally known as Croyden's Gulch. It is there that the incredible, the unbelievable manifestations began. I was there last night. I *saw* things happen. There were voices of men who had departed, there were visions and figures that would bring terror to the strongest men. Today I saw the sheriff's posse disappear into thin air. You need never expect to see Tilson or the others again. *I saw them disappear!*"

As he stopped, his listeners squirmed in their seats and looked uneasily at one another. From outside there came a faint rumble of thunder. The clock ticked through the hush.

Luther Abercrombie told substantially the same story that he'd told the sheriff earlier that evening. Finally, he set about to prove that supernatural things *could* happen. He quoted at great length from the well-known works of famous writers in the past; he showed book after book to the men and invited them to examine the passages when the meeting was over.

Lazarus who was said to have returned to life was referred to, and many other stories from the scriptures. The lawyer made a convincing talk and left no doubt in any mind about the fact that Croyden's Gulch was a place to shun. Croyden's Gulch, he said and seemed to prove, was *haunted*. Spectral figures moved about there—yet left no tracks. Men, horses, even wagons disappeared. It must have been these ghouls that had sent Rance Morgan from his grave back to the land of the living.

Then Luther Abercrombie spoke of the Lone Ranger, and the shooting of the sheriff. He did a neat job of claiming that the man who had shot the sheriff was the Lone Ranger in disguise, and said that the doctor had been about to treat and bandage the wound when the lawman had been snatched away.

In the whole of Abercrombie's story there was but one true fact: this was the statement that the Lone Ranger had been the one who took Jim Peabody from his home. Abercrombie didn't know he told the truth in that.

"I don't say there is any connection between the presence in town of the Lone Ranger and the weird events at the gulch. Perhaps the two are entirely separate. At any rate, we must do two things: We must hunt down the Lone Ranger and kill him before he can do to others as he has done to poor Hank Caulkins. We must prepare also for anything that may happen as a result of the discovery that the gulch is haunted."

"But what can we do," inquired one of the men. "We can't defend ourselves against *ha'nts!*"

"That," said the lawyer, "is the purpose of this meeting. *You must all prepare to die!*"

As if to emphasize the speech, a crack of thunder filled the room.

CHAPTER XVIII

THE SILVER BULLET

Wind carrying the breath of cold rain blew in through the windows of Luther Abercrombie's office, and fanned the faces of the men who listened with spellbound attention.

The draught caused suction in the chimney of the oil lamp so that the flame danced brilliantly for a moment, and then once more grew steady.

All the elements must have been on Luther Abercrombie's side. They furnished a perfect background for his impressive oration. Wind that foretold rain; the distant rumble of thunder; and, to fill in the pauses, the heavy, steady tick of the clock.

"I mean just what I said," the tall lawyer went on, as he rose from his chair and stood half-leaning on the desk. "We must all prepare to die."

"I'm danged if I will," bellowed one old man whose nerves were strained to the snapping point. "I never felt better in my life, till that gol-blasted lawyer started talkin'."

Someone said, "Shut up, Zeke. This ain't the time fer shootin' off yore mouth. Wait an' hear what Mister Abercrombie is goin' tuh suggest."

Zeke subsided while Luther Abercrombie eyed him coldly.

After a pause that seemed minutes long, the leader of the meeting continued.

"I don't mean to say that we are all *going* to die; I simply mean that it will be well to prepare. My intensive studies lead me to feel confident that men who are ready to pass on to another world are rarely struck down. It is those who are unprepared that die suddenly." It was pure rubbish that the lawyer talked, but the listeners by this time were in a mood to believe practically anything.

"My suggestion is that we all make out our last will and testament if we have not already done so."

His use of the first person plural was calculated to draw the men closer to the scheming lawyer.

"I'm sure that many of us have our savings hoarded away against old age. Some few may have their money in the bank, but many of you don't believe in banks. You'd sooner trust whatever hiding place you yourself had chosen. Perhaps it lies beneath the floor of your homes, possibly behind the chimney bricks; where your money is hidden, doesn't matter. The important thing is to make sure it will become the property of those who are nearest and dearest to you."

Abercrombie told the men about the value of a will. He outlined the manner in which one was made out and left in the care of someone who could be trusted— himself, for example.

"I can put all of your wills in my safe, where they will remain untouched as long as you live. If you die any one of you, then the cash you leave will be disposed of exactly as you dictate and specify."

Abercrombie paused and took a pile of blank paper from his desk. From a box he took a handful of pencils, and passed these out among the men in the room.

There was one man, standing at the back of the room, near the door, who had noticed several things about the room that gave him food for thought. There were a number of chairs and benches in the room.

Yesterday that man had been there when Abercrombie was abducted. The room had had no chairs then. Someone had provided the seats while the lawyer was at the Haunted Gulch. Someone, even then, had known that this meeting was to be called!

The stranger reasoned further: if the meeting had been planned ahead, instead of being impromptu as Luther Abercrombie made it appear, there must be some very definite purpose for the meeting. That purpose had to be connected with the story of the Haunted Gulch. In some way, it had to tie in with the supposed reincarnation of Rance Morgan.

When the lawyer had supplied everyone with pencils and paper, he explained the procedure. "It won't require witnesses," he said. "Just sign your name after you have given the location of your favorite hiding place and named the one to whom you want to leave your worldly goods. Then fold the paper so that not even I shall see it and bring it to me. I will seal it for you."

This performance, grim as it was, might have been comic if the men were not so pathetically in earnest. The stranger in the group remained unnoticed while he studied Abercrombie and thought of how the lawyer must be chuckling inwardly.

More reasoning on the part of the stranger: Why did Abercrombie want those wills? The answer—to learn just who had the largest hoarded supply of money, and where. What would Abercrombie do with that information? Of course he would pass it on to the one man who could give him orders—Rance Morgan.

Rance Morgan then, or perhaps the man who impersonated the Lone Ranger, would make it his business to kill, then rob. The blame could be placed so easily on those who would never be brought to justice.

Once Abercrombie passed on all of the valuable information that was contained in the wills to Morgan's gang there would be one of the most wholesale massacres the district had known since the Apaches had been driven out!

One by one, the townsmen shuffled to the lawyer's desk and dropped hot sealing wax on the loose edges of their documents. Abercrombie stacked the wills in a small pile beside his lamp. He looked at the men with a benign expression as if he felt that in this evening's work he was performing a great public service.

The Lone Ranger, still in disguise and seated in the rear of the office, had a sudden and a startling thought. If these men were the ones that Morgan and Abercrombie suspected of having hidden wealth, then it was almost a certainty that they were *not* members of the Morgan gang.

Here, right at hand, was an item of information that the Lone Ranger had wanted desperately. A score of men who were not Morgan's men. A score of townsmen who were in awe of the man who was thought to have been hanged! A score of men who might be counted upon to fight on the side of law and order, the side of justice, when the right time came.

The Lone Ranger planned his next act carefully. He knew that death would be the penalty for failure. He must gauge each movement against the distance; he must act with speed, and accurately. He reached into the gun belt at his hips and slipped a silver bullet into the palm of one hand. His other hand inched one of the two six-guns from the holster. He moved cautiously to avoid discovery.

Abercrombie placed the last of the wills on the pile. "Now," he said, "I will put all of these into my vault and we shall pray that they will remain there for many, many years to come. I don't care—"

Abercrombie said no more along the line he had been following. Instead he screamed surprise. A gun had barked inside the room. Glass flew from the chimney of the oil lamp on the desk. The lamp itself seemed to burst into a million bits as oil showered in the room.

Pitch darkness! Milling men who shouted in fear and anger. There were yells and cries of "Get a light.

Who fired that shot? Where's there another lamp? Someone just ran past me. Find a match. Get a light."

Abercrombie felt himself shoved violently to one side. He stumbled against a chair, then tripped and fell with a clatter, his long legs tangled with the wooden ones of the bentwood seat.

A gust of wind swept the room and blew out the first match that was lighted. Someone announcing in loud tones that he had found another lamp. "Someone git a match."

Thunder out of doors. The wind again. Stomping feet and snarls from those whose toes were walked on. A nervously held match flared for an instant and went out. Another match and this time a measure of success. The lamp was lighted, and the man who held it hurried to the desk.

"Lemme help yuh git up, Mister Abercrombie. Gosh sakes, I hope yuh ain't hurt bad."

"I'm not hurt. Give me your hand." The lawyer gained his feet. His eyes were burning with anger. "I won't permit anyone to leave this room until I know who fired that shot," he stated, looking about. "Someone obviously planned to kill me. I intend to know who it was."

There was a long pause while those in the room looked at one another. Abercrombie glanced down at his desk, casually at first, and then with an intensity that carried the eyes of others to the same point of focus.

The lawyer's jaw sagged, his eyes widened into a stare that combined surprise and fear.

The stack of wills was gone! The place they had occupied was not vacant, however. In a pool of oil from the shattered lamp, a small hard object glittered brilliantly.

Luther Abercrombie knew, without examining the object more closely, exactly what it was and what it meant. It was a bullet. A bullet of silver, solid silver. The shot that had plunged the room into darkness had come from one of the Lone Ranger's guns. *The real Lone Ranger!*

Outside the building a tall man raced along the ground on foot, with wind and the first drops of rain in his face. Beneath his shirt where they were well protected, he carried the names of men upon whom he felt that he could count—men who were not likely to be members of Rance Morgan's gang.

CHAPTER XIX

IN A MAKE-SHIFT CAMP

Despite his frantic efforts, his shouts of warning, Luther Abercrombie couldn't restore his meeting to order. Those of the men who remained were wild-eyed as they discussed what they'd heard and seen. The others had raced from the room; some to pursue the stranger if they could catch sight of him, the rest to go home and report the astounding news of the Haunted Gulch to their wives.

Abercrombie himself was on the verge of exhaustion. The nervous energy which had kept him going for the past two hours was exhausted; now he slumped into his chair, his head dropped forward, and he passed a white, blue-veined hand across the taut skin on his forehead. The doctor examined Abercrombie and insisted that he discontinue any further activity until he had taken some rest.

"You've done all you can for the present," the medical man assured him. "What you've said won't be forgotten. All of those men will be back here in the morning and you'll be able to show them that it is more important than ever that they make out their wills."

"I guess you're right," replied the lawyer. "I'll get to bed."

Rain fell steadily most of the night. It dripped from the eaves of the sheriff's home and seemed almost symbolic of the utter desolation that filled the heart of the lawman's wife. Ma Peabody had no thought of bed. Fully clothed, she sat at the shattered window of her husband's bedroom peering out into the black and mysterious pocket of the night. Her eyes were dry. The woman was beyond the point of tears.

Ma Peabody felt somehow that she had failed her husband. Could the doctor have saved his life if she hadn't insisted upon remaining in the room? She wondered about this.

Once she was vaguely aware of confusion somewhere outside. That was when the Lone Ranger made his escape from Abercrombie's meeting. She didn't know—or care—what had caused the blurred sound of excitement. Nothing mattered except the safety of her husband; she could think of nothing, but his shooting and the abduction that had followed.

Out in Croyden's Gulch rain drizzled through the dense tangle and washed out any footprints that had been made near the entrance. It streamed down the face of the gulch's steep sides and dropped a curtain over the mouth of the cave.

Inside the cave men slept peacefully on blankets that had been spread upon the floor. Rance Morgan had told them a bedtime story of his appearance with the mask. He had laughed, and so had the men, when he had explained how he had posed as the Lone Ranger.

In spite of all that the townsmen might have heard to the contrary, they now had definite proof that the masked rider was dangerous, and that he must be hunted down and killed.

"I'm not through yet," Morgan had boasted. "I've got a few more trips to make to town, an' each time I'll see to it that the Lone Ranger is blamed for one more crime."

Morgan had told how Abercrombie planned to get a will from every man of means in town. "As soon as we get those wills, or copies of 'em," he had said, "we'll not only know which men have got some cash saved up, an' how much it is, but we'll know where it's hid."

The victims would be visited in turn, and the Lone Ranger blamed for every visit.

The rain washed out the tracks that Tonto made when he drove the wagon with the unconscious sheriff out of town. It obliterated all marks that the real Lone Ranger made later when he ran from town on foot to join his Indian friend. The meeting place, which had been selected by the Lone Ranger beforehand, was two miles south of town in the bottom of an arroyo. There was scant shelter here, but Tonto had done his best to make the sheriff, now his patient, as comfortable as he could.

After unhitching Scout and Silver from the broad wagon, the Indian had raised one side a couple of feet off the ground and blocked the wheels on rocks to hold it in that position. This made a sort of slanting roof that kept off most of the rain. Fortunately there was no wind in the arroyo or the rain would have been driven in the open sides of the shelter.

Blankets spread on the ground on top of soft grass made a slightly damp but otherwise comfortable pallet for the sheriff.

Next, the Indian hurried about the arroyo with a small hand axe, and hacked a supply of dry firewood from the underpart of fallen trees. The fire he built was small but cheering, and it gave off sufficient light for Tonto to inspect the lawman's wound and apply what surgery and first aid he could.

By the time the Lone Ranger arrived, the sheriff was bandaged and fully conscious.

Tonto rose to meet the tall man whose clothes were dripping water.

"Hank Caulkins has been shot," the Lone Ranger said. "Everyone thinks the Lone Ranger did it."

The sheriff heard the amazing statement and tried to rise to a sitting posture. There was a thinness in his voice, in place of his usual heartiness. "What's that about the Lone Ranger?" he demanded.

"I said, the Lone Ranger is supposed to have shot and killed Hank Caulkins."

"It's a lie!" The statement was made flatly.

"Why do you say that?"

"Because the Lone Ranger never shot an' killed a man in his life. I'll vouch fer that."

Inwardly the Lone Ranger thanked the sheriff for

his statement; aloud he said, "You seem to be pretty sure of that."

"I am sure."

Tonto placed strong but gentle hands on the huge shoulders of the wounded man and pressed him back to his former flat-on-the-back position.

"Who do you think would have shot Caukins?"

"I dunno, but it wasn't the Lone Ranger."

"Do you know who shot you?"

"Yes. Of course I do."

"Who?"

"Luther Abercrombie."

"Why?"

"Because the dirty double-crossin' rat is up tuh somethin' that's downright crooked. I dunno what it is, but if I live tuh git back on the job, I'll darn soon find out."

The sheriff looked at the tall man who stood before him, and squinted as he tried to make out his features more clearly in the faint light from the unsteady fire.

"I dunno who you are, but yore voice sure sounds like one I've heard before." There was a perplexed look on Jim Peabody's face.

"I was with you when you were shot."

The sheriff pursed his lips. "Yuh don't look the same," he observed after a pause.

"You were in your office listening to a wild yarn the lawyer was telling. There was a lot that he said that wasn't true. Among other things, he said that he had spent the night in Croyden's Gulch. I was outside on the porch and heard him. Then I came in and gave you a note and called your attention to the fact that his stiff shirt would have been soaked limp if what he said was true."

"That's right. I remember that now."

"When you called on him to explain that fact he drew a gun and fired."

The sheriff nodded. "Right. That's about all I c'n remember for a time. Next thing I know, I was in my bunk at the house an' the sawbones was workin' on me."

"The doctor was ready to murder you, Sheriff."

"*What?*" Once more the big man tried to rise and Tonto eased him back.

"You get-um well quicker, if you stay on back."

"You'd better do some explaining, stranger. What's all this about the Doc doin' me in for keeps?"

"After he shot you Abercrombie sent out an alarm that brought a lot of men running to capture me. He planned to blame me for your shooting. Since you were the only one who could accuse him of it—you *had* to die."

"But yuh said the Doc was fixin' tuh kill me."

"The doctor has to take orders from Luther Abercrombie." The Lone Ranger went on, as briefly as he could, to tell about the faked hanging, and the vast organization Rance Morgan had called to his aid. He told about the doctor's false statement and gave the sheriff all the information he and Tonto had gained about the gang.

"Your own deputies," he said, "are working with Rance Morgan. They're not dead, or carried off by the fanciful spooks the lawyer talked about. They're in Croyden Gulch, in fact they've made it their headquarters."

The sheriff was impressed. He listened without comment. When the Lone Ranger paused, he said, "Go on, tell me some more."

"I was captured and held by Morgan in a cave in the gulch, but managed to make my escape. Morgan knows that I'm out to spoil his plans. That's why he has ridden into town with a white horse and a mask, and so aroused the townsmen that they'll shoot me on sight."

"*You?*"

Quietly, the tall man said, "Yes."

"Why you? As I understand it, stranger, it's the Lone Ranger that Rance Morgan is after."

"Perhaps you should know, Sheriff, that I, sometimes, am called the Lone Ranger."

"Jumpin juniper!" expostulated the wounded man. "You the Lone Ranger! By darn, it don't seem possible. Why I . . . aw-w-w that's just some more lies. I've listened tuh lies these past weeks till I don't figger on hearin' nothin' else. Don't try tuh fool me, mister. I'm owin' my life to you, I can believe that much. An' if they's anything I can do tuh pay yuh fer what you done, just say so. But don't try an' tell me you're the Lone Ranger."

"Then let me tell you about a meeting that was held in Luther Abercrombie's office."

"When?"

"Tonight."

"What was it for?"

"To tell the men in town the same wild story the lawyer told you: about the gulch being haunted, the posse dropping out of sight there, and Rance Morgan coming back to life. The whole thing was held to build up the townsmen's fear to a point where they'd make out their wills and leave them with the lawyer."

"Why'd he want them?"

"To help the Morgan gang."

"How'd him havin' the wills of the townspeople help the Morgan gang?"

"I'm not sure, but I think the plan is to rob the richest men in Kerr's Corners and perhaps kill some of them. Any murders, of course, will be blamed on the Lone Ranger. And the wills will show exactly who has money and where it is hidden."

Peabody snapped his thick fingers and said, "Now that's doggoned good reasonin', an' it makes good sense. I wouldn't wonder but what yer right."

"The wills were stolen, though."

"Stolen?"

The Lone Ranger nodded. "There was a shot and the lamp went out. In the dark, the wills disappeared from the lawyer's desk, and in their place was left—a silver bullet."

"*Wooooosh!*" The sheriff could hardly contain himself. His anger at the far-flung schemes of the outlaw band had been increasing as the Lone Ranger talked. He was fairly trembling with fury at his own helplessness when he learned how brilliantly the lawyer had connived to get the most confidential information from the trusting and badly frightened settlers. When he heard about the silver bullet, he almost bellowed in spite of his weakness.

"The Lone Ranger!"

"It was the Lone Ranger who left the silver bullet."

"An' took the wills?"

"It was the Lone Ranger who took the wills."

The tall man squatted beside the sheriff and held out a small bundle of papers. "Here they are. If you want further proof, Sheriff, I'll show you my gun belts, each loop filled with silver bullets."

"I—I c'n hardly believe it. L-let me see them bullets."

"I'm afraid there's hardly enough light here. I'll give you other evidence." He raised his voice. "*Here, Silver.*"

Such a pawing of the ground and snorting! The horse just beyond the edge of the tilted wagon reared high and pawed at thin air, its forefeet came down and dug the ground. The demonstration continued for a moment, but halted immediately when the same deep voice called, "Quiet, Silver."

"But," the sheriff argued, still not wholly convinced,

"if you are the Lone Ranger, what about the mask an' what about them old clothes yore wearin'."

"The rest of my outfit is in the woods near Croyden's Gulch. It would have to be there, wouldn't it? Otherwise the story I've told you couldn't be true. I couldn't come into town with the mask and the clothes Rance Morgan and the lawyer were familiar with."

Finally convinced the sheriff's manner changed entirely. He dropped his voice, his heavy form relaxed, his face lost all the harshness that had been there since the day—it seemed ages ago—that there had been an attempt to poison Bat Kester.

"Partner," he said, "I'm convinced. I—I dunno what I ever done to merit help from you. Lord knows I've done the best I could tuh keep the law around Kerr's Corners, but my work's been uphill an' the results ain't been none too good. I ain't deservin' of the help of the Lone Ranger. I can't believe I'm here, bein' took care of by you an' yer Indian pard."

"Don't try to talk too much just yet, see if you can rest. But there's just one thing I want from you, and then you're to sleep."

"Hold on, I've got tuh have my say. I had a hunch it was the Lone Ranger that was helping me out a while back, an' I was given reason tuh think so. But when I studied it over calm-like, I figgered it was just too much tuh hope for. I thought the redskin was only foolin' me; I figgered it just couldn't be the Lone Ranger, himself, that had carried off Luther Abercrombie. But now, by thunder, it *is* you. You're here tuh help me. You're goin' tuh fight on my side. I—I cain't believe it."

"Listen to me, Jim, there's something I want."

The sheriff wouldn't listen until he had finished with what was foremost in his mind. "It . . . it's like a man that's starvin' . . . he . . . he first hopes fer food, then he finds that there ain't no use in hopin', an' he gives up expectin' food. Then it gits tuh be a point of just wonderin' how long he c'n hold out an' how much the finish is goin' tuh hurt. Then all of a sudden along comes the finest meal a man has ever seen. Stranger, that's the way it is with me. I was licked. I didn't see no way on earth that I could ever rid our country of the hull of the Rance Morgan gang, about best I could hope fer was tuh get a couple of the rats. Now, when I'm wounded, when I'm thinkin' there's nothin' c'n be done, along comes one man, *the* one man in all the world that's likely tuh be able tuh help me out, an' . . ."

"Thanks, Jim. You're going to be able to count on me. Now do just one thing for me. Your wife is mighty worried about you. I don't think she'll have any rest until I can let her know that you're alive and in good hands."

"My wife! That's so. Is she all right? Have them skunks done anything tuh her?"

"No." The Lone Ranger didn't think it necessary to tell the sheriff that he felt grave concern about the safety of Ma Peabody. If Abercrombie thought the sheriff had whispered the name of his would-be assassin, her life wouldn't be worth much.

"I want you to write a note that I can take to her and tell her that she's to trust me."

"Yer concerned about her worryin'." The sheriff sighed heavily. "Yuh want tuh put her mind at ease, is that it?"

"Yes."

"If I'd had any doubts about you bein' the Lone Ranger, that one thing would wipe 'em away. Who else would be ready tuh head back tuh town . . . just tuh keep a woman from worryin' about a fat old galoot like me."

The sheriff's eyes were moist and not from rain. He reached for a stubby pencil in the pocket of his shirt. His hand brought out a little notebook with a pencil. "I'll give you that note—Lone Ranger," he said.

CHAPTER XX

GRAY DAWN

At dawn the rain gave way to gray mist that fogged the town and seeped in through open windows and gave everything it touched a clammy feeling.

The rocking chair in which the sheriff's wife had spent the night was silent, its squeaking stopped as the exhausted woman dozed.

She was a pathetic figure when the Lone Ranger saw her through the broken window. Her head had drooped until her chin was almost touching her chest. Her mouth was slightly open. One hand hung limply beside the chair and the reddened fingers with large bony knuckles were mute evidence of her life of hard and heavy work.

Her hair, once black but now streaked heavily with gray, was still loosely knotted in the back but wisps had strayed across her forehead. Drops of dew or mist had formed to gleam like a jeweled halo on the chimney of the oil lamp that still burned steadily behind her. The hand in her lap held a handkerchief in relaxed fingers.

The Lone Ranger stepped through the window without awakening the woman. For a moment he watched her with a suspicious tightness in his throat. Her night of worry had been caused by him, by his abduction of Jim Peabody. Yet what else could he have done? Softly, barely audible, the voice of the Lone Ranger murmured, "I'm sorry."

He bent and placed gentle arms about the woman. He lifted her bodily from the chair and carried her to the bed. He tucked a pillow beneath her head and drew a blanket over her.

Ma Peabody sighed deeply. Her chin quivered for a moment. Then she turned her head on the pillow with her eyes still closed.

Watching her, the Lone Ranger was surprised to see how small and frail the sheriff's wife was when in repose. He could hardly believe that this was the same woman who had fought with the ferocity of a tigress in behalf of her wounded mate. He debated the idea of waking her to gladden her heart with news that Jim was going to return when his wound had healed. He decided to let her sleep till she was rested.

He drew a folded paper from the pocket of his rain-soaked shirt and placed it beside the woman's head where she could hardly fail to see it as soon as she opened her eyes. Then the Lone Ranger silently slipped out the window.

Silver was waiting not far from the house. The Lone Ranger mounted and rode out of town.

This was the beginning of a day that might bring almost anything. Forces were gathering in Kerr's Corners, forces motivated by the outlaws in the gulch.

They might remain subdued for several days, but sooner or later there seemed bound to be a series of tragedies that would practically wipe out the best blood in the region, and leave the accumulated wealth and natural resources to a band of criminals whose ambition and greed was likely to carry them to even wider depredations.

It was good to ride through the early morning coolness. Silver welcomed the activity and covered the ground with great, free strides. The Lone Ranger studied the leaden sky; he judged that the rains were over and that another hour would bring the sun and constantly increasing warmth until the heat became intense. Thought of the promised temperature for the afternoon made him able to forget the chilly discomfort of his wet clothes.

He reached the woods and broke through the trees, wet leaves slapping at his face and hands. Arrived at a clearing, he swung from the saddle.

It took but a few minutes to uncover his other clothes which had remained quite dry within the protecting tarpaulin. Less than five minutes after his arrival at the clearing, the Lone Ranger was once more in the saddle and riding back to the arroyo to join Tonto and the sheriff.

It would be good to be dressed in his more familiar attire. Even though Rance Morgan had made the Lone Ranger the quarry of man-hunters, he would feel more at ease with the mask and the well-fitted clothing.

There was little to be risked by the change. His disguise had made him equally sought after.

Tonto grinned as he saw the Lone Ranger slip the mask in place. "That much better," he said. "Now sheriff know you Lone Ranger."

"I'm still somewhat concerned about the sheriff's wife, Tonto. I wish there were some way we could guard her," the masked man said as he settled his hat in place.

"Mebbe me go there. Keep-um watch."

The Lone Ranger shook his head. "By this time, I'm afraid the Morgan men will be after you as much as they are me. They'll shoot either of us on sight."

"You not watch-um wife of sheriff?"

"I have been thinking about her. I think we can make sure she's watched." The Lone Ranger glanced at the sheriff and noticed that the big man slept.

"How long before it will be safe for him to go back to town?"

"Mebbe tomorrow. Mebbe two days."

"It depends upon how quickly his wound heals, is that it?"

The Indian nodded.

"In that case, we can't wait." The Lone Ranger took up the wills and opened one after another of them. He came upon the will of a man named Frawley, Chet Frawley.

"This is one of the men who came to Hank Caulkins's place just after the shooting last night," the masked man explained. "He's one of the wealthiest men in the town, has a big ranch, and hires about ten hands. He impressed me as the sort of man who would go a long way to defend what he owns."

Tonto listened attentively.

"Chet Frawley, as I understand it, was one of the closest friends the sheriff had. He has a will that leaves his wealth to about a dozen relatives, and the sums of cash he mentions are pretty important."

"What you do about him?"

The Lone Ranger explained a scheme that brought a wide grin and a nod of approval to Tonto's face. Seizing the bridle, the masked man mounted. He called out, "Hi-Yo, Silver! Away-y-y!" as he raced toward town.

Chet Frawley was a well-knit man of middle age. His bullet-shaped head, bristling hair, and stubborn chin marked him as a man who would be hard to argue with if he were convinced that he was on the right side. He stacked his plate with its second burden of pancakes and flooded the fragrant pile with syrup.

"I don't take much stock in what that lawyer had to say," he growled to his wife across the table. "Just the same, I figure it ain't a bad idea for every man to make a will."

"You could leave the will with me, an' tell me where you've got your savin's hid, Chet."

Frawley shook his head emphatically. "Too much

risk for you. What with the sort of outlaws we got 'round here, I wouldn't put it past 'em to try an' make you tell what you knew. They'd likely torture you if need be, to make you tell what they wanted to know. If its known that you ain't got any idea where my cash is salted down, you'll be a darn sight better off."

Frawley packed a big wedge of breakfast into his mouth and chewed vigorously.

"Who d'you think stole those wills last night?" asked the woman.

"Dunno."

"What about the Lone Ranger?"

Frawley looked up sharply. "What about him?"

"I heard that he was the one that shot poor Hank Caulkins. Do you think he might have been the one that stole the wills?"

"Some say so, some say not."

"How's that?"

Chet crammed his mouth again, and bolted the food before he replied. "Well, there was the silver bullet. That would make us think the Lone Ranger got the wills. On the other hand, there wasn't anyone around the office that was dressed like the man that shot Caulkins, an' *that* was supposed to have been the work of the Lone Ranger. Now you figure it out. You're as good at figurin' as I am."

"What d'you plan to do?"

"See Abercrombie this mornin'."

"And then what?"

"Leave a will an' testament with him, then clean my shootin' irons, stock up my men with plenty of ca't-ridges, an' wait fer whatever comes next."

Chet Frawley looked up from his plate and saw a wide-eyed expression of panic in the face of his wife. Her eyes were set on something that must have been behind him. Chet dropped his knife and his hand streaked to his hip as he swung in his chair.

"Steady!" The word snapped like a whip. "Don't go for your gun, Frawley."

Frawley's hand froze where it was.

"Get your hands on the table and keep them there. I'll let you turn this way, but turn slowly."

Frawley saw the tall man at the door; the white sombrero of fine quality and, just beneath the hat's broad brim, the *mask!*

"I'm not after your money," the masked man said "You needn't look so startled."

"Me? Startled? Why drat your hide I—"

"Save it!" The Lone Ranger's voice was crisp and commanding. "I heard that Sheriff Peabody's wife had come here to hide. What about it?"

"Well?" barked Frawley with severity that matched the Lone Ranger's, "what about it?"

"I'm not taking any chances on her telling too much. I've come to take her on a little trip. Where is she?"

Chet Frawley's face was a study. After a long pause the masked man spoke again. "I'm waiting, Frawley, where is Mrs. Peabody?"

"Have you looked at her house?" asked the rancher slowly.

"No. I was told that she'd come here to avoid capture."

Frawley paused again. Then he said, "What if I don't tell you where she is?"

"I'll simply have to tie you and search the house."

"That's about what I figured. I can see there's no use trying to deny anything to you. Ma Peabody *did* come here."

The Lone Ranger could have shouted his pleasure. Frawley was all that he had hoped he might be.

"But," went on Chet Frawley, "she ain't here now."

"Where is she?"

"Look, stranger, I heard what happened to Hank Caulkins and I don't want none of that sort of murder to happen in my house. I'm a man that knows when he's got to tell the truth. Now Ma Peabody came here an' I was willin' to do what I could to take care of her, but she didn't feel it was safe to stay here. She figured this was too close to town. She knew you'd be huntin' for her, so she rid out of here before daybreak an' headed for Joe Frisby's place. That's about five miles further out from town. You know where it is?"

"I'll find it," the Lone Ranger said. "But if you're not telling the truth, Frawley, I'll be back and settle with you."

The door closed on the masked man and a moment later a clatter of hoofs could be heard. Frawley leaped to the window and looked out at the figure that already had gone beyond the range of a pistol shot and was rapidly increasing the distance.

"Chet, what did you tell such lies for? You know Ma Peabody wasn't here an' she didn't go to Frisby's place. That masked man'll be back here with both guns blazin'."

Chet nodded. "I know. I asked him if he'd looked at Ma's home an' he said he hadn't."

"But—"

"We can't let Ma Peabody get captured. I'll get over there as fast as a horse'll take me an' take my best men with me. We'll get Ma an' fetch her back here. Then we'll have some men with guns tuh guard her. By juniper, if that masked man comes back, we'll be ready to welcome him with plenty of gun smoke."

The Lone Ranger didn't ride far in the direction of the Frisby place. He rode only far enough to get out of sight of anyone on Frawley's ranch before he swung in a wide circle to head back around the town to the arroyo where Tonto waited.

"Chet Frawley," the masked rider muttered as he rode, "is just what I hoped he'd be. Now we can be certain Ma Peabody will be guarded."

CHAPTER XXI

BORROWED WILLS ARE RETURNED

"Now that your wife will be protected, I can tell you what I've done," the Lone Ranger said to the sheriff when he reached the arroyo camp.

Jim Peabody listened with keen interest to the narrative, and heartily approved of the masked man's choice of Chet Frawley and the strategy he had used.

"There ain't a squarer shootin' man this side of the Mississippi," he said emphatically. "I've knowed Chet fer a mighty long time an' I'm glad yuh went tuh him."

"I thought it best that your wife not be left alone. Now there's something else I want to discuss with you, Sheriff."

"Go ahead. If they's anything in the world I c'n do tuh help yuh, Lone Ranger, jest say the word." Jim chuckled softly for a moment. "Can't help thinkin' about Chet Frawley. He'll be movin' Ma tuh his place tuh guard her from you. I wonder what he'd say if he was tuh find out that's just what yuh wanted him tuh do."

"There'll be a lot for you and Chet Frawley to talk

about when this thing is finished. But it's a long way from finished now."

The sheriff grew sober. "That's what's got me beat. I don't see how in blazes you c'n do anything. Probably half the town's in cahoots with Morgan."

"It's possible that he has a lot of men who are taking orders from him, but I think most of them will desert him when they see he's on the losing side."

"Then what?"

"Once you can be sure that the laws will be enforced by honest deputies, you'll be able to get some action. First of all, we want to explode that story about the gulch being haunted, and prove to everyone that Rance Morgan was never executed. Too much superstitious fear has been planted in the people's minds by Luther Abercrombie."

The sheriff frowned. "Abercrombie," he snorted. "That buzzard is goin' tuh be aplenty hard tuh jail. He knows more tricks than a red fox."

"He doesn't know enough to stay honest," the Lone Ranger said. "He can't be so very smart."

"A darn sight smarter'n the men that'll have tuh prove him crooked."

"Well, we'll see about that when the time comes."

The Lone Ranger drew the wills from his pocket and showed them, with the seals broken, to the sheriff. "You know everyone in town. I wish you'd look these over and tell me which of these men you feel are strictly on the level."

Peabody had been fixed in a half-sitting posture by Tonto. He thumbed through the papers hurriedly, looking only at the names that were signed to them.

"Offhand I'd say that all these boys are on the level. They're all men that've lived here for a long time, an' worked hard; I've seen most of 'em start up from nothin', an' build a little herd of livestock that gave 'em a livin'. They're good, God-fearin' men that provide good homes fer their wives an' young uns. They ain't a man here that I'd suspicion of anything crooked."

"That's what I hoped you'd say."

"Why?"

"I hoped that Luther Abercrombie had invited only men of that type to his meeting. Apparently he didn't send for any of Rance Morgan's men."

"What's the difference?"

"It shows that he was after the information that is to be found in these wills, and that's why I'm going to see that he gets these papers all back again."

"You mean," the sheriff demanded in surprise, "you're going to take all these wills back tuh that crooked lawyer?"

The Lone Ranger nodded.

"Then why in thunder did yuh take 'em in the first place?"

"I had a plan in mind."

"But now," the sheriff protested, still uncomprehending, "you're takin' 'em *back*."

"I might as well. Chet Frawley and all the others

seem to think the lawyer is on the level; they think it's a good idea to leave their wills in his care. If I don't return these wills, the men who made them will simply make out new ones. Why not save them that trouble?"

Jim Peabody scratched the back of his neck reflectively. He muttered, "Don't seem tuh make much sense tuh me. Risk yer neck gittin' 'em, now you'll likely risk it again takin' 'em back."

There was the trace of an enigmatic smile on the portion of the Lone Ranger's face that showed beneath the mask. Jim Peabody's sharp eyes saw this.

"You got somethin' up yore sleeve."

"I'm counting a lot on human nature, perhaps I'm counting too much. I hope not."

Jim Peabody watched what followed with keen interest. The Lone Ranger called Tonto to help him and for over an hour the two men worked industriously over the collection of last wills and testaments.

If the masked man felt any compunction about the things he did, he must have thought that his acts were justified because he showed no hesitancy. One after another the papers were worked over, Tonto making cautious erasures and the masked man making deft strokes with a pencil.

Finally the Lone Ranger returned the papers to the sheriff. "Now look them over and tell me what your first impression is."

"I know," the lawman said, "that you been makin' some changes in these wills, but I'm hanged if I can spot 'em. You done a right neat job of it. I can't see nothin' at all that's wrong with 'em."

"Study them."

The sheriff's lips were pursed as usual when he concentrated. After a few moments he said, "I allus thought Bart Baxter had more'n fifty dollars hid away. Shucks, that's down right disappointin'."

He read through the next. "This here is funny, Pete Larkin has led me tuh believe that he could lay his hands on a right big sum of cash if ever the need arose. Now I see here that he claims he's got about one hundred dollars in gold cached beneath the floor of his house in the southwest corner, an' he wants tuh be sure the hull of it goes to his wife."

The reading and the comments went on in the same vein for some time. The lawman indicated his amazement on several occasions until he came to the will of Chet Frawley. Then he expelled the air from his lungs in a windy exclamation of amazement.

"Whew! Did you note this?"

"I saw it."

"Why doggone Chet Frawley! Here he never let on that he'd come intuh cash of this importance. I figgered that he put what cash he had intuh buildin's an' livestock. Why the close-mouthed old son of a gun, I'm hanged if he ain't got a couple of fortunes salted down against his old age."

"Good enough, Sheriff. That's all I wanted to know."

"Huh?"

The masked man took the papers from the sheriff. "You," he said, "have told me all I want to know. You have come to the conclusion that no one has enough money to make a robbery worth while except Chet Frawley."

"Yep, but—"

"I'll get going now. I want to return these to Luther Abercrombie before he begins replacing them."

"Yuh don't dare show yerself in town. Yuh'll be shot on sight."

"I'll try and avoid being seen."

"Yuh can't do it.

"Then I'll have to try and dodge any shots that are fired."

The Lone Ranger whistled sharply once, and his big white stallion leaped toward him from the tender grazing in the center of the arroyo.

"Stay with the sheriff, Tonto, and see to it that he doesn't try to get back into action too soon." The masked man stood with one hand on the saddle. "I'll be back as soon as I can."

"Me watch-um."

A foot in the stirrup, and Silver was under way. A cry from the masked rider, and the horse became a shaft of white that streaked beneath the morning sun across the level land between the arroyo and the town.

Luther Abercrombie's ordinarily forbidding expression was even more so as he entered his office. He had wakened almost as tired as he had gone to bed, and would have welcomed more hours of sleep had he dared to take them. This, however, was to be a busy day, and he must not waste a moment of it.

He scowled heavily about his office, recalling the sudden loss of the wills he had schemed so carefully to acquire.

Rance Morgan would be expecting those confidential papers, or at least a copy of the information they contained. Now it would be necessary to replace every one of them—if he could.

Abercrombie, as well as Morgan, knew the folly of attacking the settlers on the strength of what they *seemed* to own. Cattle, horses, buildings and land were not easily negotiable when stolen. Cash was. It was cash that Morgan was after. Cash first, because with ready money there went power. Only by securing duplicates of the wills could the hidden wealth become available.

The lawyer's office was a sorry sight. The air was still heavy with the tobacco smoke of the preceding night. The floor was littered with bits of paper and tracked with mud. Pieces of glass from the shattered oil lamp crunched beneath the lawyer's boots, and a spot was dark and moist looking where the lamp's oil had been soaked up by the dry boards.

Luther Abercrombie sat down heavily in his chair. He leaned back, pondering on the best way to replace the wills. Should he wait and count on the fears of the men to bring them to him, or should he go out and solicit them? The best means might be a combination of the two. Perhaps if he had the doctor go about and suggest that certain picked men again call upon the lawyer—.

A creaking door punctuated the lawyer's thoughts with a period. He looked up quickly, then snapped forward in his chair. He half rose before he noticed the black hole in the barrel of a gun that was pointed squarely and unwaveringly at his face.

Above and behind the gun, the lawyer saw a mask. He heard a voice say, "Steady, Abercrombie. I'm here to talk to you."

"Y-y-you! You're the . . . the one they call the Lone Ranger."

"That's right." The masked man stepped closer to the desk. "There are a few things we should discuss."

Abercrombie was badly scared at first. When his first fear had passed and he recalled the fact that the Lone Ranger never shot to kill, he regained some of his composure. "What do you want here?" he said.

"There seems to have been a mistake made, Abercrombie."

"What do you mean?"

"You were taking wills from the men who were here last night." It was a statement, not a question from the masked man.

"What of it?"

"Someone took the wills and left a silver bullet in place of them."

"Well?"

"Don't you have any idea who that man might be?"

"I can guess," replied the lawyer coldly. "There's only one man who's trademark is a piece of silver cast in the shape of a bullet."

"Perhaps you also know that someone around here has been assuming an identity that doesn't belong to him."

The lawyer stared steadily at the keen gray eyes that gazed at him with equal steadiness through the slits in the mask.

The Lone Ranger went on. "I don't like to have people do things that might make *me* a hunted man. I usually find some way to stop that sort of thing."

Still Abercrombie stared without replying.

"Please don't think I'm making an empty threat or saying anything that might be construed as a warning. I simply made a statement. You can take it for what it is worth and pass it on to anyone you care to. That is," he paused, "if you know of anyone who might be interested."

The lawyer found it hard to keep his surprise from showing in his face. He listened to the voice which spoke with such fine modulation, and a command of the English language that matched his own. Here, he thought, was a strange adversary—a dangerous one. Rance Morgan had been right in feeling that the Lone Ranger must be eliminated.

"As I said, Abercrombie, someone has been giving

the wrong impression around town. There is at least one man who has used part of my identity, there may be more than one. I don't know. At any rate, the wills of the settlers were stolen from here last night and a silver bullet left in their place."

The masked man held his gun in one hand while with the other he reached beneath his shirt and drew out a package which he tossed on Abercrombie's desk.

"There," he said, "I'm returning the things that were taken. I think the place for them is in your safe."

"Do you mean to say you didn't take them yourself?"

"Did I say that?"

"Well, not exactly that."

"I said there was someone around here who needed suppressing. I said those papers were taken from here last night and a silver bullet left in their place. You now have the papers back. You might keep the silver bullet. Call it a souvenir, if you like. I have unearthed one impostor. If you know of any other impostor, hand it to him."

During the last part of his speech the masked man had been backing to the door. He opened it, stepped through, and shut it quickly behind him. A second later the lawyer heard him cry, "Hi-Yo, Silver." Hoofbeats receded rapidly.

The lawyer snatched at the papers, looked at the first few. "I don't understand it. Is someone else posing as the Lone Ranger? It wasn't Morgan who was here last night. Then who in the name of mercy was it? And—*what has the real Lone Ranger done to him? How did the real Lone Ranger know? What else does he know? Why did he return these wills to me?*"

The lawyer's mind was in a state of wild confusion. He was plagued with unanswerable questions. Only one point stood out clearly: He had again the papers that were so eagerly desired by Rance Morgan.

And Morgan was waiting for them, in the cave at the Haunted Gulch.

CHAPTER XXII

ABERCROMBIE'S END

Rance Morgan held a council of war in the cave at Croyden's Gulch. Those of his men who were supposed to have dropped out of existence, victims to the mysterious forces of the gulch, sat about the cavern listening attentively to what their leader said.

"We've got to depend on Abercrombie to a certain extent, but I don't trust him too far. I got an idea that smooth-talkin' lawyer figgers he'll go as far as he can with us, then turn us in."

"I had about that same idea," said Jack Tilson, the erstwhile deputy. "We know doggoned well that the lawyer ain't honest. He's already proved as much. Well, if he'd double cross the sheriff an' everyone that's trusted him, he'd double cross us just as quick, if he saw money in it."

"Glad to hear you feel that way, Tilson, you'll be a good man for what I got in mind tonight."

"What's that?"

"I'll get to it in a minute. First of all, I want you all to know just what the plans are."

The others shifted to more comfortable positions in the pause that followed.

"In the first place, boys, we won't have to put up with the discomfort of this cave forever. We will have to put up with it fer a few days though, maybe for a few weeks. But that all depends."

"Depends on what?" asked one of the men.

"On how things go. Last night I went into town fixed up to look like the Lone Ranger. I made a plenty big show for Hank Caulkins's wife, an' by now everyone will be huntin' for the masked man, alive or dead. That redskin that got the horses away from us needs killin', too. That's why I'm figurin' on takin' Tilson into town with me tonight."

Morgan turned toward Jack Tilson. "You're about the same size as that Indian pard of the Lone Ranger."

Tilson nodded. "I been expectin' them two would be comin' back here to see what's what."

"If they do, we'll be ready for 'em. Now tonight I've got to call on Luther Abercrombie. You'll dress like the Indian an' come in with me."

"Why call on Abercrombie?" someone inquired.

"He's supposed to have some papers for me—the last wills an' testaments of some of the men in town. I gave him the names of the men."

"What good are the wills?"

"Plenty good. They'll tell me which of the men around here have enough cash hid away to make it worth while callin' on them. Those papers should tell us where the cash is hid, how much of it there is, an' everything else we want to know."

Admiration showed on the faces of Rance Morgan's followers.

"If that don't beat all."

"I never heard the like of the schemin' Rance can do."

"By ginger, that's the slickest thing I ever did hear."

There were other comments of a similar nature, all of which brought a satisfied smile to their leader's brutal face.

"I don't stop with gettin' that information," Rance Morgan boasted. "Jack Tilson will be along. When we face the lawyer gent, we're fixed like the Lone Ranger and the Indian—and *we drill Luther Abercrombie.*"

"Kill him yuh mean?"

"Yes."

"Fer keeps?"

"Why not?"

No one could think of any good reason for allowing the lawyer to live. By nightfall he would have served his purpose and done all Morgan expected of him. Abercrombie, anticipating cash rewards—and probably planning a double cross when he found a way to cash in on it—would be paid off in lead.

"Jack Tilson will do the shootin' this time. We may's well fix it so the Lone Ranger's pal will get shot on sight as well as the Lone Ranger."

There were nods from the men. Someone said, "What about the rest of us?"

"That's right, Rance, I'm plumb wore out from sittin' here an' doin' nothin'."

"You men'll get all the action you want by an' by.

Meanwhile, just sit tight an' amuse yerself with cards."

"But what about you appearin' as the ghost of Rance Morgan?" It was Tilson who spoke. "Thought yuh figgered that you could use that ghost business tuh mighty good advantage?"

"And I can. If anyone comes nosin' around here, we'll give 'em a scare they won't forget. But as long as I can palm myself off as the Lone Ranger by riding around in an outfit like his, I may's well do it, and let that masked hombre take the blame fer things I done. Later, maybe, I'll have tuh go out as my own ghost. We'll see as tuh that."

"What about the hosses on the plateau, ain't there some chance that they'll be spotted an' traced to us?"

"Anyone comes near here will be shot. That's why we keep guards on hand all the time. It won't take but a couple of shootin's tuh make folks give this region a plenty wide berth, if they don't do it now. With the story Abercrombie told though, I don't look fer much curiosity on the part o' the folks from town."

There was more talk, most of it a rehash of plans, and a discussion of the hopes and prospects for the future. The day dragged slowly for the men. They played poker endlessly and without much enthusiasm. Their meals had to be simple because they had been unable to carry with them much of a stock of food. They were, however, willing to undergo present discomfort and hardship for a future that looked so bright.

It was a curious contradiction that, while there was

money enough in the cave to buy any and all the luxury and ease the outlaws could want, yet they must, for the present, endure discomfort, boredom, and insufficient food. So far, the profits of their crimes had bought nothing, and yet they schemed and plotted to increase their fortune many times over.

The doctor and the others in town, who stood ready to help the Morgan gang, when called on, were not considered important enough to discuss. At least none of them was ambitious enough to seek the things that made the killers suspicious about the lawyer.

Somehow the day ran out and, shortly after dark, Rance Morgan and Jack Tilson scaled the ladder to the top of the plateau, where they exchanged greetings with the guard who was voluble in his admiration of their disguises. Selecting horses, they set out for town.

Morgan knew better than to risk being seen as he entered town. He would dispose of his work in the lawyer's home first, then allow himself to be seen making a noisy escape that would depend on surprise for its success. And once more there would be a frantic hue and cry for the death of the Lone Ranger.

"These horses ain't too much tuh brag about," said Tilson as the two approached the rear of the row of houses. "They'll have tuh do, though, till we can find some that're better."

"Yours is a paint and mine is white. That's the main thing. Folks ain't goin' to notice much closer'n that."

"Ain't that the back of the lawyer's place?"

Rance Morgan said it was. They rode close, and dismounted.

"He's expectin' me, he won't raise no alarm when we go in."

"That's good," replied Tilson who wore the buckskin of an Indian.

Morgan slipped a mask over his eyes, pushed open the unbarred door in the rear of the house.

Luther Abercrombie was in his library. He looked up without surprise when he heard the approach of the masked man and grinned slightly. "You sure don't look much like the real Lone Ranger when you're in the light."

"Why not?" asked Morgan testily, taking the comment as something of an insult. "What's the matter with this get-up?"

"Oh, there's nothing in particular that's wrong with it, Morgan, it's just the personality you give to it. That, however, doesn't matter much since a rear view is about all that anyone will get when you leave here."

He looked past Morgan at Tilson. "What's the idea of the Indian disguise?"

Rance Morgan ignored the question. "You know what I'm here for. How about it?"

"It? You mean *them*. I have the wills right here and waiting for you, but you'll find you were away off on your guess as to whom were the best prospects for robbery."

"How's that?"

"Morgan, the sum total of the wealth you estimated is correct, but instead of being distributed among a dozen or more men it is all held by *one* man."

"Who?"

"Chet Frawley."

"So much the better. Does his will say where the cash is hid?"

A nod from Luther Abercrombie.

"All right, then, we'll shove on. You do your act now, Tilson."

Abercrombie looked up to see the gun that Tilson held. "What's that for?" he asked. He saw the look in Tilson's face. "You can't mean—"

The few people who were in the street heard a shot and a sudden wild scream of frenzy that ended in a gurgle. They stopped and wheeled toward the direction of the sound.

The next instant there came a clatter of hoofs. Two men raced into view and dashed out of town before anyone could gather wits enough to draw and fire. All that was known, was that a pair of men had thundered away from the lawyer's home; one was masked, riding a white horse to which he shouted, "Hi-Yo, Silver," while the other wore the outfit of an Indian and rode a paint horse.

In less than five minutes, a mob was gathered in the lawyer's home. The lean man, with parchmentlike skin, lay sprawled grotesquely on the floor, and in the center of his forehead there was a small, bluish hole where the bullet had gone in.

Luther Abercrombie was dead. There was no question about it. The news spread through town like wildfire, and again there was an angry cry of, "Get the Lone Ranger."

CHAPTER XXIII

THE START OF A SHOWDOWN

Jim Peabody had become a problem to Tonto. The big lawman felt so far on the road to recovery, and so concerned about the safety of his wife, that he wanted to go home that very night.

"I don't give a hang what the Lone Ranger said," he grumbled, "I'd still feel better about Sara if she was home with me there tuh stand guard than I do with her over tuh the Frawley ranch. Dad-rat it, Tonto, I'm goin' home."

"You stay here," said Tonto. "Wound not healed yet."

"Yuh got the bullet out an' a bandage on me. Shucks, I'm all right. Just put this wagon back on four wheels an' hitch a hoss to it an' lemme go."

Tonto was firm in his refusal. It was the private opinion of the Indian that Jim Peabody really would be better off at home with his wife than in the arroyo with his worries. The Lone Ranger, however, had said that the sheriff must be held, at least until his return.

Tonto busied himself with unnecessary chores about the camp so he could pretend not to hear the constant rumbles of complaint that came from the bulk of man beneath the tilted wagon.

A short time after dark the keen ears of the Indian caught a distant shout that came from the direction of the town. He cocked his head and listened. There were other shouts, then a sustained clamor.

Tonto frowned and glanced at Jim Peabody. By the light of the tiny campfire he could see the sheriff propped on one elbow, perplexed wrinkles on his forehead as he too bent an ear toward Kerr's Corners.

The cries of men subsided, but a new disturbance took their place. Hoofbeats! Fast hoofbeats that approached from the direction of the town. Only the mighty Silver had the speed to make that pounding rhythm.

The Lone Ranger and the white horse dropped from the high bank of the arroyo to the camp. The masked man leaped from the saddle. "How's the sheriff?" he barked.

"Him get well heap fast."

"Just how well is he?"

"I'm well enough tuh git outen this cramped place an' go home where I belong. Doggone it all, Lone Ranger, can't yuh see I'm fit tuh be tied an' all wore out with sprawlin' here on the ground?"

"His voice sounds strong," the masked man said to Tonto.

"Him get strong quick. Not lose much blood."

"What about his wound? Will that heal if he moves about tonight?"

"It'll heal if yuh let me go an' git my wife. Just h'ist

me intuh this wagon an' lend me a hoss an' lemme go, won't yuh?"

"It might," replied the Lone Ranger, "be a good idea."

The masked man stepped to the side of the sheriff and crouched. "Peabody, there's a pile of trouble in town. That lawyer, Luther Abercrombie, has been killed."

"Who done it?" asked the lawman without showing much surprise.

"The townspeople think I did it."

"I ain't askin' what they think. I'm askin' you who done for Abercrombie."

"I'm fairly sure it was Rance Morgan."

"I savvy."

"He and another man. There were two in town tonight, one was dressed like Tonto."

"He sure is fixin' things so's it'll be unhealthy fer you to be seen around here, ain't he?"

"He probably feels he has to. The main point is that he *did* call on Abercrombie. That means he probably has possession of the papers I left with the lawyer."

"An' what will he do next?"

"Peabody, I have an idea that Rance Morgan isn't going to waste time. That's why I would like to see you moved tonight. That is, if Tonto is sure it won't affect your recovery or cause your wound to become infected."

"You got a scheme in mind, eh?"

"Perhaps."

The sheriff studied the masked man for a full sixty seconds with eyes that were most penetrating and appraising. Tonto stood near the Lone Ranger, waiting for whatever might be the next move.

"If you got somethin' that needs doin' that I can be of help on," Jim said slowly, "yuh needn't bother to ask Tonto if I can be moved. I'll tell you that I can be. I'll tell yuh more'n that: I'm goin' tuh be moved or, by thunder, I'll move myself."

There was a quick nod from the Lone Ranger. "The sooner we get started the better," he said.

He went to one corner of the heavy wagon and lifted it so the wheels were off the rocks that held them high off the ground. Tonto pulled the stone aside. Then the same operation was performed at the other end of the rig and the wagon was in its normal level position once more.

While Tonto backed the horses, Silver and Scout, on either side of the singletree, and tossed the harness over their backs, the Lone Ranger talked, "We'll take you to Chet Frawley's, Peabody. You will find your wife there. Frawley will have a lot to say about the Lone Ranger. You will understand that."

Jim Peabody grinned. "Whatever he says, I'll know the inside facts."

"You'll have to give Frawley a pretty serious talking to before you can convince him that he must help us."

"I can do that, too." The sheriff was vital and alive

now that he didn't have to anticipate another night in the crude shelter of the tipped-back wagon. "I'll convince Frawley that the moon's made of green cheese if you say that's what I got tuh do."

"You won't need to go that far," the masked man said, "but you will have to convince him that I'm not the man who killed Hank Caulkins."

"Sure thing. Yuh ready fer me to climb aboard that wagon now?"

"I'll help you up."

"You'll do nothin' of the sort. I can't make the grade climbin' into a saddle, but when the day comes I can't get this stomach of mine onto a wagon, I'll quit sheriffin'."

It was a larger task than Jim Peabody supposed, to get into the wagon. His weakness surprised him when he got to his feet, but he was determined to do all that he could to aid the Lone Ranger in whatever the masked man chose to do.

Tonto leaped to the seat after tossing the blankets and other equipment to the rig and then the Lone Ranger swung to the back of Silver. It would be easier to guide the horse from this position than it would be from the seat of the wagon.

He was about to start when the Lone Ranger heard the sheriff call out, "Hold on, partner."

"What is it, Jim," the masked man called over his shoulder.

"You told me about Rance Morgan an' his men bein'

in the gulch. Well, what I don't savvy is, why we don't take a posse and go there an' clean the gulch out."

"It wouldn't do. In the first place, there are lots more of Morgan's men in Kerr's Corners. In the second place, there must be a real showdown. If we found Tilson and the others in the gulch, they'd have a story about being prisoners there, and it would be almost impossible to find any charges that would hold them in jail or send them to the hangman. When we clean out this county, we want to make a thorough job of it."

"You're the boss, whatever you say is all right with me."

"Hi-Yo, Silver," the masked man's voice rang out. "Away!"

Two horses dragged the jouncing wagon from the arroyo and raced across the plains.

The Lone Ranger didn't go through town. He cut around Kerr's Corners in an arc that took him to the Frawley ranch without being seen by any of the townsmen.

Jim Peabody seemed to feel stronger as the trip progressed. The man's rugged health had made his recuperation a speedy one. Activity, instead of tiring him, seemed to be the very tonic he needed.

The wagon and the horses clattered to a halt near the ranch house. Two armed men on horses approached warily to find out who the visitors might be.

"We can't waste time talking to them, Tonto," snapped the Lone Ranger. "Give me a hand."

Tonto knew exactly what was required. His fingers fairly flew as he unbuckled harness straps, tossed blankets and saddles in place, and cinched up. As the cautious Frawley ranch hands eased closer, the Indian and the masked man mounted and dashed away.

Jim Peabody was alone as the waddies came up and halted. He met them with a broad grin on his face.

"Peabody!"

"The sheriff."

"What you doin' here?"

"Who rid off?"

"What horses was those two?"

"Boys," replied the lawman to the impetuous questions of the cowhands, "I ain't got nothin' tuh say right now, but you give me a hand inside that house, an' I'll tell things that will sure as shootin' make yer hair stand up on one end." As an afterthought he said, "Is my wife in there?"

She was. Jim was helped from the wagon, and escorted from the horseless wagon to the house.

Meanwhile, the Lone Ranger and Tonto pushed their horses to the utmost.

"Come on, Silver," the masked man cried in the night.

"Gitt-um up, Scout," shouted the Indian.

Both men felt that this night would bring the showdown. Every event pointed to it: the death of Luther Abercrombie, Rance Morgan's possession of the wills. It wasn't Morgan's nature to postpone what could be secured at once, not when it was money that was concerned.

The Lone Ranger's surmise was accurate. Rance Morgan gathered his men about him in the cavern hide-out and quickly sketched his plans.

CHAPTER XXIV

CALM BEFORE STORM

Pale moonlight flooded the plateau and the small group of horses that grazed there to make a scene that was deceptively peaceful. An instant later, however, it became a scene of wild activity, of running men, of shouted cries, and horses that raced madly under cruel spurs.

Rance Morgan's men scrambled up the rope ladder from the gulch. Morgan still wearing the outfit that resembled the Lone Ranger's was in the lead as the outlaws fanned out toward their mounts.

Morgan's promise of the rich booty to be had for the taking at Chet Frawley's house gave added speed to the men's feet.

Rance Morgan himself made a beeline for the white horse. He paused beside the beast and shouted to his men. "Remember, there's likely to be a passel of cowhands at the Frawley place, so don't waste no time in thinkin'. Shoot first. We'll do the thinkin' afterwards."

Morgan put one foot in the stirrup. The horse must have been unusually eager, nervous perhaps, because his weight had no sooner touched the leather than the horse lunged forward.

Morgan was taken by surprise, but he had a grip on the horn that saved him. He swung his right leg up and felt himself almost pulled into the saddle by the speed of the horse.

It wasn't until then that Morgan realized that he was in a strange saddle. It was much finer than his own, more comfortable, too. He hadn't a chance to study it, however. The horse was pounding along madly, already far ahead of the rest of his gang.

Morgan heard the men behind him shouting to slow down.

"Wait fer us!"

"We cain't keep up with yuh."

"Slow down, Boss."

Morgan yanked back heavily upon the reins, cursing wildly at the white horse. The harder he pulled, it seemed, the more the horse ducked its head into the wind and fairly flew ahead. Morgan braced his feet against the stirrups and sawed at the reins. But he had all he could do to stay in the saddle. "Blast yer hide," he cried, "slow down!"

His cries had no effect on the plunging horse as it sped along.

Panic filled the outlaw's very soul when he became fully aware of his position. This was not his own white horse; no horse he had ever ridden had the speed of this silver streak of white. He was on the fastest, the most powerful horse in all the West. Rance Morgan, who wanted to be looked upon as the Lone Ranger, was riding the mighty stallion Silver. *The Lone Ranger's horse.*

He couldn't understand it. He didn't try to. He held on, knowing that a spill at that speed would be almost certain death.

It couldn't be Silver! Hadn't he tried before to mount that horse and failed? How had Silver happened to be in the place of his own white horse? Why had the stallion permitted him to mount, before bolting away like a flash of lightning, only straighter.

Morgan didn't know that the Lone Ranger himself had placed the stallion there. He didn't know that the figure he saw riding ahead of him was Tonto, whom the stallion followed.

Rapidly the white horse overtook the Indian, cutting down the space between them with each long, powerful stride. Morgan's eyes were wide and wild with panic. He knew he should draw his gun, be ready to fight, but he didn't dare loosen the hand that clutched the saddle horn in his fear of being thrown from the horse's back.

Now the horse and rider approached a clump of sycamores. Tonto, less than fifty feet ahead, was already lost to view beyond the first of the trees. Suddenly Morgan, too, was in the grove, a miniature woods. Another instant and he broke through into the open plain beyond.

That was when it happened.

Morgan had just realized dimly that the Indian was not in sight when he heard a sharp, shrill whistle. Silver slid to a halt that threw Rance Morgan over the lowered head of the horse and sent him sprawling and rolling on the ground. Another whistle, and an answering whinny from Silver.

Dazed from the spill, Rance Morgan was only half aware of the things that happened in the next few seconds. He caught a hazy glimpse of a tall man wearing a mask who stepped from the trees, he felt the weight of something on his chest. An Indian straddled him, and tossed ropes about his wrists, while the masked man jammed a gag into his mouth.

The next instant, Morgan was lifted bodily and dragged into the small clump of trees and tied there. The rest of his men dashed into, then out of the woods.

"Hold on." A heavy voice cried above the hoofbeats.

Jack Tilson and the others reined up quickly, wheeled their horses and came toward the masked man who forked the white horse.

The moonlight was shaded by the trees. The Lone Ranger was in the shadows when he spoke to Morgan's men.

"It won't be safe for me to go into town in this outfit again tonight. Everyone'll be in an uproar about the death of Luther Abercrombie."

The Lone Ranger made his voice as much like that of Rance Morgan as he could. None of the men seemed to detect any difference. They had no reason to suppose that in the few seconds it had taken them to overtake the leader, the real Lone Ranger had displaced him.

"I'll head straight for the Frawley place and get the lay of the land. You men go on to town and round up every one who can be trusted."

It was odd, the use of the word "trusted." The Morgan followers interpreted the meaning as the masked man meant they should.

"I just remembered that the sheriff's wife is at the Frawley place and it's likely there'll be a lot of extra men there on guard. We won't take chances tonight. Get every one of the boys; then head for the ranch as fast as your horses will carry you. If you don't see me there, dismount and wait near the house. Don't shoot until you're shot at."

The men nodded that they understood. Tilson said, "I'll feel a darn sight better with the rest of the men along with us. Frawley hires some pretty darn good gun slingers."

"Get going."

"Right." Tilson led and the others followed along the trail to town.

The Lone Ranger was playing a dangerous game. It might very well end in grim tragedy for a score of people unless his judgement was correct. He hoped that Tilson and the others who had been in the gulch were trusted members of Rance Morgan's gang and that they would know the identity of the men in town who would fight on their side.

He also counted heavily upon the ability of Jim Peabody to persuade Chet Frawley to follow instructions.

"We'll have to wait a little while," the masked man said to Tonto. "Those men can't ride roughshod into town. They'll have to go in quietly and speak to the right men secretly. That may take some time."

Tonto looked concerned. "You take plenty big risk later on."

"I'll have to depend on Silver, Tonto, but I've counted on him before."

"But you go to town," said Tonto. "You let all feller take-um shot at you."

"There's no other way. If they hit me, I'll have to depend on you to patch me up."

Tonto gave his attention to Rance Morgan's ropes and made sure they'd hold the killer helpless. The Indian heartily disapproved of the masked man's habit of undertaking the most dangerous tasks alone.

It was suicidal, this plan of the Lone Ranger. What chance would he have, riding through Kerr's Corners so shortly after the murder of Luther Abercrombie? Why every man in town was armed and waiting, in fact praying for the chance to kill him.

Luck had been kind to the Lone Ranger thus far. Each carefully woven thread of his plan had fitted into the pattern. The outlaws, confident that they could make their big clean-up in a single attack on Frawley, had grown reckless. After tonight, they could ride away from the gulch. There was no one else in town worth robbing. They had, therefore, disregarded the fact that their tracks could be followed across the plateau to the gulch. What the people in Kerr's Corners knew or suspected wouldn't matter after the hold-up—the Morgan gang would have moved to other parts.

No one in town noticed the arrival of men who were supposed to have disappeared in Croyden's Gulch. The men themselves saw to that. Each of the group that had been with Rance Morgan drifted slowly into the crowded area, threaded his way warily between rows of buildings, and sought out a friend.

"Rance need's yuh," was the word that was passed. "Tell the ones you can trust about it, then drift out of town. We're meetin' on the trail between here an' Chet Frawley's place."

A nod of understanding, and the men would separate.

This was an act that was repeated many times in Kerr's Corners that night.

While the air was filled with nervous, excited speculation about the Lone Ranger and the death of lawyer Abercrombie, men with set expressions on their faces slipped into their homes. They loaded up their guns and gun belts with fresh cartridges, saddled fresh horses, and rode out of town as quietly as possible.

Men came in two's and three's to join the shadowy group that waited on the trail.

Tilson met them and whispered a brief explanation as he turned to wait for other recruits.

Finally Tilson decided that no more men would be

coming. He signaled them forward and led the way at a trot toward Chet Frawley's ranch.

But the Lone Ranger had seen the outlaw band start out. He moved on silent feet toward his horse which had been tethered dangerously close to town.

"Now," he said, slapping the silken neck of the big beast, "it's time for us to move, Silver. I don't know how we're going to make out. It's not fair to risk your life, along with my own, but it has to be that way, old fellow."

The stallion muzzled the masked man's sleeve. It was as though Silver understood each word his master said.

"We might as well get started, Silver." The Lone Ranger took one moment longer to inspect his guns, then jamming them back in their holsters, he mounted and rode toward town.

He appraised the town's one street ahead: there were a lot of men milling about. Lots of horses, too, all of them tied to hitch racks in front of the saloons. Many of those men had already ridden out, an hour or more before, in angry search of the man they thought to be the Lone Ranger. Now they were talking about the masked man.

Another moment, and they would *see him.*

CHAPTER XXV

BATTLE

The Lone Ranger grew tense as Silver moved slowly toward Kerr's Corners. He was almost abreast of the first of a long row of buildings. Less than fifty feet ahead a group of men stood in the light from the open door of a saloon.

The masked man drew back on the reins and Silver halted, then looked back at the man in the saddle as though to ask, "What now, master?"

The Lone Ranger patted the horse's sleek neck. He knew what was ahead of them. He must run the gauntlet twice. Race through the town, then turn and race back in defiance of those who dared think they could shoot him. He must goad them to pursuit. From the rising and falling back of his running horse, the Lone Ranger must be ready to shoot with such accuracy that he could disarm a man on either side of him who looked likely to shoot with disastrous results.

He felt the string of his mask, making sure it was snug; he gave the front of his white hat a slight tug to settle it lower on his forehead. He was ready. "All right, Silver. This is it!"

Silver stepped forward. The masked man lifted his voice in a loud cry that rang to the far end of town. "Hi-Yo, Silver! Away-y-y-y!"

The horse exploded into full speed. A vivid flash of white swept through the street. A dozen men turned, stared, then yelled and snatched at their guns.

"Come on, Silver!"

Men streamed from saloons on both sides of the street. Bootless men in stocking feet, some shirtless as well, rushed from their homes. Windows flew open, shutters slammed back as sleepy-eyed folks showed their heads and cried out in alarm.

The Lone Ranger himself had a gun in each hand, his reins were dropped loosely over the pommel of the saddle. Flames leaped from the masked man's guns while deliberate cries of scorn burst from his lips.

Wild yells, raging curses and empty threats made a din that was augmented by the sharp bark of pistols and the heavier roar of rifles. Glass crashed from windows that were struck by wild shots.

Half a dozen men were shouting orders, a score more were racing for their horses by the time the masked rider reached the far end of the town.

Guns, whinnies of fear from the horses, screams of women who had heard of the Lone Ranger and the murders charged against him in Kerr's Corners, hoarse shouts of men, clattering hoofs, frantic but clumsy efforts to mount and pursue, stomping hoofs, smashing glass—and then above all these, a ringing voice in the distance, "Hi-Yo, Silver! Away-y-y!"

The Lone Ranger swept into view, charging through the street with utter disregard for the barking guns.

The men, some of them in their saddles, were re
and swung into the road behind the hard-ridin
masked man who crouched low over his horse's back.

The chase was on. This time it was different than
before. The Lone Ranger was still in sight when the
men took up the pursuit. Previously, the masked man
who had killed Hank Caulkins, then Luther Abercrombie, had been out of sight almost before the chase
got under way.

Out of town, into the open prairie land, out across
the plains, the masked man rode. He glanced back and
noticed that a horde was following. "Come on, Silver,"
he cried, "we've got them on our trail now. We've run
the gauntlet and they haven't gotten us yet. We'll lead
them a chase they will never forget."

On through the night the masked man rode, his
followers holding doggedly to his trail. He kept the
pace steady, but held down Silver's blazing speed so
that those who came behind would not become discouraged and abandon the chase.

There was bitterness in the Lone Ranger's heart as
well as exultation. Those men who rode after him, he
knew, were men who loved honesty and justice. They
were men who rode in hate to capture one whom they
looked upon as a killer.

None of Morgan's men were in that pack behind
Silver's flashing hoofs; Morgan's men were somewhere
ahead. Only those townsmen who had not been sum-
moned by Jack Tilson were ones who truly opposed

crime and criminals. The Lone Ranger's strategy had at last succeeded in sorting out the good men from the bad.

An occasional shot barked, but, for the most part, the pursuers knew the range was too great for effective gunplay.

Far ahead Chet Frawley's house was the scene of another kind of activity.

Jim Peabody sat in Frawley's favorite chair, insisting that the Lone Ranger was a "darn good friend fer a man tuh have," and saying, "you jest wait an' see."

The lawman's wife was near him, smiling happily now that Big Jim was near her.

But Chet and his wife were still not wholly convinced about the Lone Ranger. "I always thought he was a mighty straight shooter," the rancher said, "but he certainly sounded downright menacin' when he come in here with those demands of his."

"You fetched my wife here, didn't yuh?" asked the sheriff. Then at a nod from Frawley, "Well, that's just what the Lone Ranger wanted you to do. You try an' figure out any other way that he could o' persuaded you to do that same thing."

"Maybe so," admitted Chet grudgingly. "After hearin' how the Lone Ranger had shot up poor Hank Caulkins, I'll admit I wasn't feelin' any too social about him."

"That's the whole thing. Rance Morgan has been raisin' hob around town, just to get the folks steamed up into huntin' down the real Lone Ranger. The reason is as plain as day—Rance is downright scared of the Lone Ranger."

The sheriff had already explained all he could about Rance Morgan, the gang in the gulch, and the Lone Ranger's plans. In response to his request Chet Frawley had called his cowboys to the house and they were, at that moment, assembled in one room and waiting for whatever came.

"If this plan works out," Jim Peabody went on, "we'll have the whole pack of the rats trapped. There won't be just a couple of 'em jailed, an' the rest still at large to set 'em free. There won't be a dozen men ready to swear to lies on the witness stand, or help fake a hangin' so killers can laugh at law an' order. If the Lone Ranger—"

Jim Peabody never did get around to finishing that speech. Gun's roared; first in the distance, then nearer and nearer until the big house fairly shook with the vibrations of gunfire from outside and the answering fire from the front room.

Chet Frawley was on his feet, racing through the door to his men. "They comin'?" he cried.

Their blazing guns were his answer.

The outlaws not only were coming, they were coming fast. A man on a white horse led, a mob of others followed.

"Remember," yelled Chet Frawley. "Don't shoot that man on the white horse. Let him come in here. Let him get here safe. Drop those rats that are comin' behind him."

Guns and more guns. The air in the house reeked with the fumes of exploded gunpowder. Windows were gone with the first volley. The women of the house had been barricaded behind timbers too thick for bullets to go through.

Chet snatched his rifle from a corner and fired into the mass of men that swept toward the house.

Jim Peabody's big frame filled the doorway. "I'm in on this," he bellowed.

"Get back you old fool," shouted Chet. "You've got too much carcass. You're too easy to hit."

"I'm in on it," retorted Jim, stubbornly. He crouched near a window and rested the barrel of his six-gun on the sill. He fired. "That's one for Bat Kester," he yelled.

Jim fired again and had the satisfaction of seeing the man he had aimed at, drop from the saddle, roll over several times, and lie still. "That squares things for Hank Caulkins."

Frawley was frantic. "Get away from that window. Three men can fire from the space you take up, Peabody."

"Maybe so, but three men won't drop no more of them varmints than I will. I got scores to settle an', by darn, I'm goin' to settle 'em." His gun barked and jumped again. "That's fer Abercrombie even if he was a skunk."

The door burst open. The Lone Ranger leaped into

the room while Silver scooted around to the far side of the house without a rider. The masked man slammed the door and shouted, "Hold your fire!"

"What for?" barked one of the cowboys.

"Stop firing, I'll tell you," came the sharp reply.

"Do what he says," ordered Chet Frawley. "The Lone Ranger is in charge from this point on."

The firing in the house was stopped but there was gunplay going on stronger than ever outside the house. A pitched battle was being fought. The Lone Ranger explained briefly:

He had dashed up to the men of Morgan's gang, ordered them to charge the house, then raced ahead of them to join Chet Frawley and the sheriff. Meanwhile, the townsmen who had followed him had run into the band of outlaws—and the fight was on.

"Now that you know there are friends as well as enemies out there, be careful how you shoot. You might hit the honest men."

"See here," roared Frawley. "See all that fightin' goin' on out there an' me an' my boys out of it. 'Tain't right! Come on, boys, let's help with the clean-up." His men followed Frawley from the house.

CHAPTER XXVI

CONCLUSION

Frawley and his men on one side, the townsmen on the other, made a perfect trap for Morgan's men. The fight was short and sharp, and the end was inevitable. Half a dozen of the outlaws who hadn't been blasted from their saddles, threw down their guns and threw up their hands. There were loud cries of surrender which Chet Frawley heard, and gave commands to accept.

An hour after the last shot had been fired, the Frawley house represented a combination jail and hospital. The wounded outlaws were bandaged, the others roped. Sheriff Peabody was in his glory, busier than he had ever been, and rising manfully to the occasion. He barked orders to his deputies, and he swore in a dozen new deputies.

Many of the men from town who had pursued the real Lone Ranger laughed heartily when their mistake, and the masked man's ruse, was pointed out. They discussed his feat in glowing terms while Ma Peabody and Chet Frawley's wife passed among them serving coffee in big mugs.

The Lone Ranger himself, however, was waiting outside. He still wasn't entirely free of all suspicion. There had been a number of the townsmen who looked curiously at him. Then at last the Indian, Tonto, rode into view on Scout leading a white horse with a man in the saddle.

"You were a long time coming, Tonto."

"You finish fight too soon," grinned the Indian. "Tonto come when fight all over. That what you say. Me wait. Now come."

Those inside the house saw the door swing open and a tall man stumble across the threshold. The door closed.

"What's happened to the Lone Ranger?" cried Ma Peabody. "He's hurt." Then on closer inspection she cried, *"He's gagged and tied."*

Knives flashed out to cut away the gag and ropes. Men hauled the tall masked man to his feet, then Jim Peabody stepped up.

"Now, by thunderation," said the sheriff in a voice that boomed with vigor, "I'll show yuh the crook that's been posin' as the Lone Ranger."

He snatched away the mask. "Rance Morgan!"

The killer blinked at those around him. Hate and rage made his eyes red-rimmed and bloodshot. His lips curled back in a snarl that was ugly.

"We got you this time, Morgan," Peabody stated, "an' when we hang yuh for the murder of Hank Caulkins an' Luther Abercrombie, the rope'll be fixed *right*. Yer whole gang is here to keep you company, an' I reckon there'll have tuh be aplenty of hangin's because the jail won't hold yuh all."

Frawley moved close to Rance Morgan. "Let me look at him," he said. Then a moment later, "So this is the *fake* Lone Ranger, eh?"

Outside there came a cry. "Hi-Yo, Silver! Away-y-y!" Hoofs pounded and faded away.

"An' there goes the *real* Lone Ranger," Frawley added. "There sure is a difference."

Ma Peabody stood at the window and saw the tall man with the mask astride the white horse riding off against the moonlit sky. Tonto rode beside him. She glanced at Jim, her husband. She saw the look of relaxation that made his face light up in a way she hadn't known for many, many months. She looked back to the plain again and touched her fingers to her pale lips. "There," she breathed, "I've blown you a kiss, Lone Ranger. May God bless you."

Be sure to read the next Lone Ranger Story:
"The Lone Ranger Traps the Smugglers"